"Christy Leigh Stewart's I surprisingly emotional powerhouse of writings that reveal the author's quirky, often irreverent wit. With unexpected insight, she exposes the uncomfortable and pulls the lid off the acceptable. Artist Megan Hansen's edgy, contemporary illustrations couple brilliantly with Stewart's prose to make this a book that you just may find yourself reading more than once."

-Lisette Brodey, author of Crooked Moon and Squalor, New Mexico

"Bold, broad, and beautiful. And pretty freakin' disturbing sometimes. The writing and art are somehow raw and refined all at once. I like it."

- Kevin Shamel, author of Rotten Little Animals

"If Zen is a finger pointing at the moon, then Christy Stewart's Loath Letters are a finger pointing at the booger on your shirt. Only, there's no booger. And you have cancer. READ IT."

- Jess Gulbranson, author of Antipaladin Blues

"Loath Letters is funny, angry, dark and honestly disturbing. Christy Leigh Stewart's words and Megan Hansen's illustrations play off each other with the terrible precision and glee of two cats dissecting a bird of paradise."

- Bill Glover, author of Tearing the Veil

"Loath Letters takes us into the darkness that lives in humanity sometimes. A collection of short stories told from the teller's point of view, it lured me into the psyche of those who could be bad or good, but essentially were human. No matter what emotion it drives you to, it will haunt you long after you are done reading it."

-Pamela K. Kinney, author of Haunted Virginia: Legends, Myths and True Tales and From Under the Moon: Spectre Nightmares and Visitations.

"Loath Letters is a fantastically naked book that wriggles under your skin. It's akin to finding a hidden diary and absorbing someone else's secrets although you know you shouldn't. Rarely does writing feel so honest and fantastical at the same time. Congratulations to

Christy Leigh Stewart for making me feel so delightfully uncomfortable."

- Matthew Revert of A Million Versions of Right

"Stewart's bite sized, tweetsized fictional petit fours are great for those who appreciate Deep Thoughts with Jack Handey and the comedy of Steven Wright and Demetri Martin and Hansen proves herself an adept and fun illustrator. An attractive fun, sweet little package...not unlike it's naughty little vixen creators"

- Garrett Cook author of Murderland Part 1:h8, Murderland II: Life During Wartime and Archelon Ranch

"It's a very bizarre collection. I read it as almost a series of confessions, some of them sardonic and funny (these were my favorite), some of them sad, some of them violent."

- Andersen Prunty, author of The Overwhelming Urge, Zerostrata, Jack and Mr. Grin, The Beard, Market Adjustment and Other Tales of Avarice, Morning Is Dead and The Sorrow King

---

"Letters, voices, shouts of anger and cries of regret … each conveying short, dark and disturbing tales of rage, tragedy and horror … examples of what some humans are capable of."

- John Walker, author of Wrath and Remembrance, Comparing Scars, Hitting Back, God's Soldiers, Hank Shank VIII, Blood and Water, Backlash

"Christy Leigh Stewart is the O. Henry of transgressive lit."

- Bradley Sands, author of It Came from Below the Belt and My Heart Said No, But the Camera Crew Said Yes!

Loath Letters

ISBN 978-0-557-27439-0

Copyright © 2009 Christy Leigh Stewart
Cover Illustration Copyright
© 2009 Megan Hansen

This book is a work of fiction, as are the characters and settings. Any similarities to true life events and or persons are purely coincidental.

Furthermore, this is not an autobiography in any way shape or form and so your prayers aren't necessary.

Dedicated to all the Drama Queens and Suicide Kings.

-Christy Leigh Stewart

I'd like to dedicate this to all the under motivated, lackadaisical, procrastinators out there. Working on this book made me miss being one of you.

-Megan Hansen

hypnotized.

els. Singing. Always singing.
laughed at me and they
yourself. For your parents and
, because they love you, so they won't suffer any-
e. They said a dark angel would come. I've been wait-

Somewhere in the back of her mind, she was aware of a dog barking.

SUSAN LISTENED HARD, trying to figure out where the dog was. Sound seemed distorted, trying to filter different through the swirling snowflakes.

"This way," Parkhurst said.

She lengthened her stride to keep pace with his. There was a luminous quality to the falling snow. The footing was slippery and the crunch of their boots sounded like an advancing army as they slogged beneath branches, each with snow, that closed overhead like a long black tunnel.

The dog barked again, closer. Slipping and stumbling, she followed Parkhurst. He stopped, placed a cautionary hand on her arm. Ahead was a dim glow of light.

Mouth close to her ear, he whispered with small puffs of warm air, "I'll circle around." He drifted away, almost immediately lost in the swirling snow.

Cold air burned her lungs. She felt she was struggling without gain as she weaved around trees, trying to move quietly and cover distance quickly. She couldn't hear anything over her own heavy breathing.

Then she stopped, and stared.

Ahead in the small clearing, a flashlight resting on the ground gleamed through the dark like a beacon. Boards were gone from the well. Two dark figures, heads covered, crouched beside it, provoking the image of renegade monks performing ancient prayers.

I'm From The Future

I'm from the future.

No one believes me when I tell them this. They sometimes ask me to prove it.

Even if I could tell you something monumental that happens in the distant future to validate my claims, we would have to wait until it happens for you to believe me.

By that time, the conversation would have lagged for so long that we might have forgotten what I had told you in the first place.

It's not fair to treat it like a joke when someone tells you "I'm from the future." To you it might seem silly, but for me it's very lonely. So far, I haven't met anyone else like me. It's not like being an ethnic minority or being disabled. There aren't support groups for me to join.

If people don't write me off at first, everyone wants to know what time I come from. They always laugh when I tell them.

I'm not years from the future, not months, nor days.

I'm from 0.025 seconds in the future. Each moment, 0.025 seconds in the future.

You can see me and hear me and interact with me, but I am already 0.025 seconds ahead of you.

That might not seem like that much of a time difference, but that's because you don't know any better. You don't see things the way I do. You don't understand things the way I do.

You live in the present. The time where things are new and the future is full of endless possibilities. The decisions you make and relationships you have are malleable.

My present is set in stone. By the time your saliva is beginning to make food bolus,

I'm already dissatisfied. By the time you've turned on the TV, I'm already bored. By the time you've said you love me, I've proven you wrong.

So you might not be able to fathom it, but I *am* from the future.

Disbelieve me all you want, but for fuck's sake, stop calling me Space Man.

About Our Date

From: Angellica Irving

Sent: Tue 12/16/08 3:42AM

To: John Tilmont

I wanted to apologize. So I got your email from Stacy; I hope you don't mind. I wont be sending you fwds or anything, I just thought I should explain myself.

When you walked me to my door and leaned in to kiss me, I didn't mean to offend you by turning away, but I'm very self conscious. I know you had already figured that out considering I mentioned it a few times at dinner. That alone makes me wonder why you were attempting to kiss me at all. I know you didn't feel anything for me, and that there was no spark between us.

I know you think I talk too much and that I'm too fat and my eyes are too far apart and that I embarrassed you. I know that you haven't thought of me once since our date even though I constantly daydream about what would have happened if I had let you kiss me. Maybe you would have come in with me and we would have slept together. Maybe you would have laughed at how badly I kissed. Maybe you would have known that my third grade teacher touched me inappropriately. In the end of every scenario you always end up holding me in your arms and tell me that everything my father said about me was wrong. I'm sure you only tried to kiss me because Stacy asked you to be nice to me. She set us up on a blind date because she knows I'm alone and that I feel envious when everyone in the office talks about their lovers or spouses and that she's seen me crying in the bathroom.

    Anyway, I also wanted to apologize to you about not being completely truthful. When I told you my last boyfriend raped me, it was a lie. I wanted you to think I was pretty, so I figured if you thought someone else found me desirable you would become jealous. The truth is, I've never had a boyfriend.

I hope you don't think I'm some sort of stalker for emailing you out of the blue like this. I just wanted to explain some things. If you didn't have too terrible of a time, I would love to go out with you again. I swear I can be a little less anxious and I would love to see you once more. I've already forgotten what your hair smells like.

Oh My God, You Guys!

I'm one of those people you've heard about on TV.

I'm that angry and disgruntled teenager that goes to school and shoots everyone.

Well, I will be. Very soon.

As we speak I'm making my plans. Making a list. Checking it twice. All that shit.

My problem is, though, that there have been SO many school shootings that people know what to look for. Dark clothes, rock/metal/goth/emo/whatever music, psychopathic drawings on text books, dark poetry, and on and on and on...

I've got it figured out though. I know how to make everyone unsuspecting. They might not even see it coming when I'm standing in front of them, shooting them like fish in a fucking barrel.

My first advantage: I'm a girl.

No one expects this kind of shit out of us because we're... I don't know... Nurturing? Because we have babies? But what about all those chicks who get abortions or kill their babies or abandon their kids or leave their kids or rape their kids or sell their kids or... Whatever, no one will see it coming, in any case. If I have my vagina to thank for that, then being called a cunt shouldn't be an insult.

The second advantage: I'm a girl.

I'm not some dumb fucking boy with a gun fetish. I've thought this out.

Rock music may be good and all, but if listening to it will give anyone ANY inclination I'm going to murder them, then I'll go without. I listen to The Jonas Brothers. I have posters of them on my wall. I have their image as my desktop wallpaper.

I masturbate to Googled pictures of them. There are no holes in my façade.

I may feel moody but I don't need to wear black or dye my hair black or wear black makeup. I have no undergarments that aren't thongs. I don't have one top that doesn't show at least one areola. I don't have skirts that don't expose my genitals. I don't have pants that won't display my thongs. No one would see me and say "That's someone who's planning to shoot me in the face." Hell, they probably wouldn't even expect me to run in this shit. But I can. I've been practicing.

I have a lot of pent-up rage I need to get out, sure, but I don't need to get it out through poetry or journals or something else someone can figure me out with. I'll wait and let out my rage when I'm killing everyone, what could be more relaxing?

I do have my lists though, of people I don't want to miss. People I won't let escape. The girls, I have listed in my notebook under "Best Friends" and the guys names I write everywhere. I write them after my name with a plus sign or in a heart. I've even given some of these guys blow jobs in the school bathrooms.

They'll never see this coming.

Domestic Abuse

When we fight, and I mean REALLY fight, I feel like none of it's really happening. The pain I'm feeling dulls and it's as if I become so disconnected that I'm just standing off to the side, watching the abuse.

I can see us just as we are, physically, when I'm watching, but it feels like I don't know those people. Who's that woman being beaten? Who's that man who has her by the back of the head, pounding her face into the floor boards?

It gets so bad sometimes.

It just doesn't seem possible to me that we are in this situation, at least not to my rational mind. When I think of us, I picture us watching TV, doing bills, tucking the kids in at night. Those everyday menial things. Not this insane scene I see before me.

We aren't those people, are we? We love each other and this sort of abuse doesn't happen in relationships like ours. The fighting isn't part of our real life. It's something we wont speak of, even immediately afterward. And I forgive you just as fast.

I know you don't mean to hurt me. I know you've had problems as a child, that one family member touched you and another one hit you. I know your outbursts aren't about me, but about you. So how can I blame you?

I'll do anything to help you. I'll do anything to remind you of who you really are and what you're worth to me. I just wish you didn't force me to hit you so hard.

The Player

I have my fair share of women.

They come in and out of my life all the time, but I wouldn't consider myself a player, and don't think anyone else does either. I don't demean these women, not at all. I care about each one in their own way, even if we're together only a night.

It's not just sex for me, which is a misconception. It's much more than that, but it's hard to explain. It's the companionship, if even for that short time. It's the excitement, and perhaps danger. It's the unknown, really, that must be the most enticing part.

When I'm with these women, I am face to face with one of the essential parts of life, and exploring it is intriguing, erotic. I am at awe each moment, with each touch and each taste. Truly, this can't be just sex. There must be another word to describe this type of melding and intimate act.

Necrophilia doesn't cut it either. It seems like such a nasty word, used by people who don't understand. And my heart goes out to those people, and I wish them luck in life, because it can't be easy to live, not knowing what it is to die.

But I do, because I've been up close to it. Smelled it, tasted it, fucked it. Been inside and outside of it at the same time. Known it for it's stark truth, both grotesque and beautiful.

I Could Love You More

Watching you sleep, as I'm doing now, is my favorite moment between us. Your face is so still and almost malleable. In this state, you can be anything I want you to be.

Most women want to change something about their partners. That's so well known it's become a cliché in comedy. Many of my friends wish their boyfriends were smarter, funnier, richer, more generous (in and out of bed), and of course, better looking. I never thought those things of you, not once.

It doesn't matter to me if you have money or not, if you went to college or are fast-witted, and you are always more then competent in bed. Your looks don't matter to me; you are always most handsome when you make me feel loved, so my attraction to you is mostly psychological anyway.

What I've always wanted is a romantic story. Most little girls want a fairy tale prince, I think, but I want a touching story that is far more romantic. I want to hold you in my arms not knowing what will come in the next moment. I want to carry you with me in my heart and remember you when it's raining, or when it's sunny, or whatever weather it was when we were last whole and happy. I want you to die.

I want to watch you fade away from a terminal disease while I comfort and support and love you. I want our love to be so deeply rooted in this sorrow that I'll never be able to get over it and your memory will never die. I don't want memories of falling out of love or slipping away; I want your life passing through my fingers like sand as I grasp desperately at them.

When I see you eating well or working out, I think of this. It's a daily reminder of what I won't have when you live life like a vivacious and healthy young man. I'll never be able to love you like I want to, and so sometimes I think I can't love you as fully as I could.

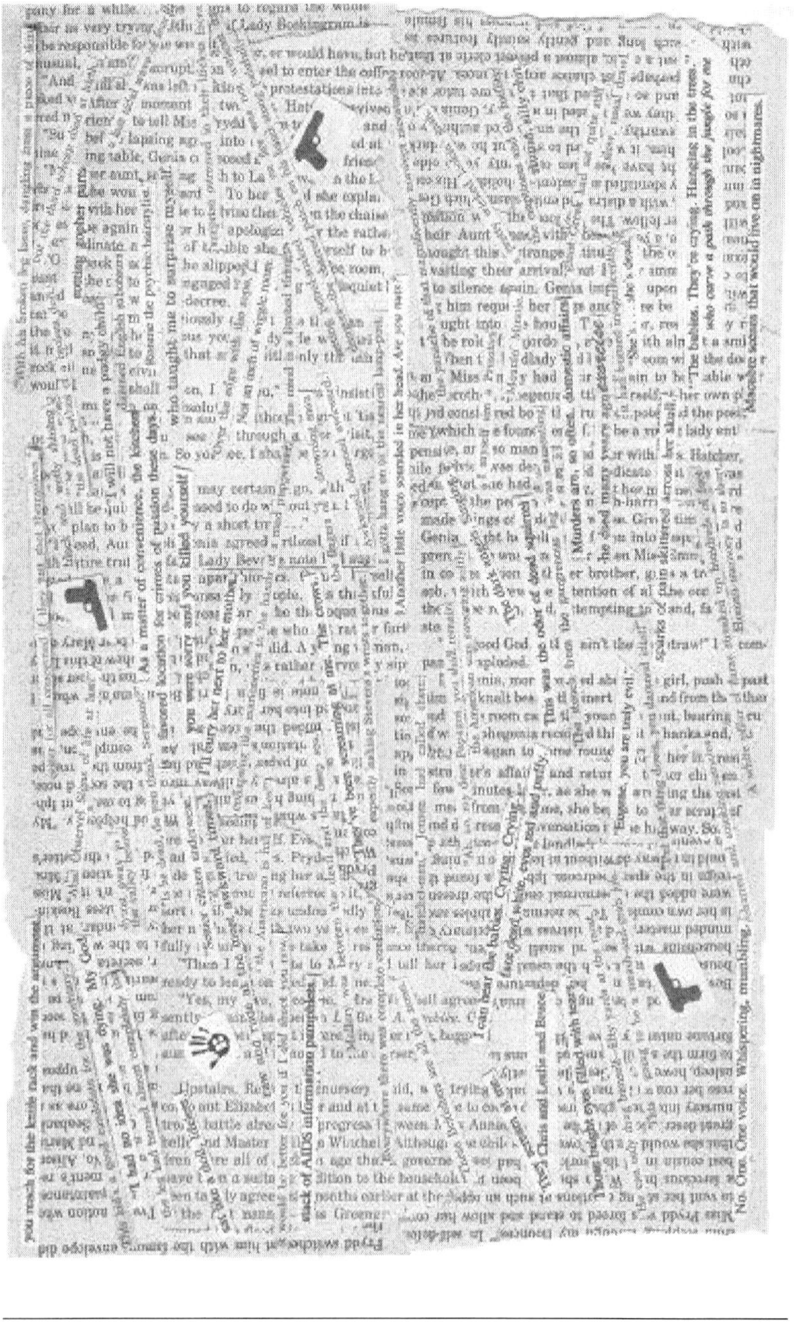

23

<u>Stupid</u>

He said he loved me and I fell for him.

He called me stupid and by that time I couldn't get away from him.

Feeling his ribs like this, bare and slick, I want to described it in some poetic way but all I can think is "this is stupid."

It strikes me as funny. As stupid. This whole situation. I find I can't stop touching him anymore.

I've felt it all before. His tendons, muscles, fat, even arteries. But, this is the first time I've seen it from the inside.

He bleeds so much, breaks so much, tears so much.

How weak.

How stupid.

I wish he could see how stupid he looks right now, so I reach for his eyes and show him.

Breast Cancer

"Welcome back," Bethany says with that friendly and empathetic smile. She wants to hear all the details and offer her condolences but doesn't know how to breach the subject.

I want to receive her condolences but I would rather watch her tiptoe around the subject for a while, maybe a few days. I want to get as much enjoyment out of this as possible. "Thank you," I tell her with my regular smile. I'm appearing strong and in control. I'm a hero, in that non-heroic sort of way. The new age sort of way that makes people who make public evidence of their personal sacrifices with a modestly brave face heroic.

"Is there hot coffee?" I ask. This abrupt subject change means I want to be treated like I always have. This makes me more heroic and later Bethany will tell the our coworkers how strong I'm being. They'll feel even more empathetic.

"Sure, I was just going to get some for myself."

Bethany is so uneasy about the situation it's taken her this long to notice. Her smile falters as her eyes trail down to my chest. There are inserts for your bra but I don't have one. In fact, I'm not wearing a bra at all. I'm purposefully wearing a form-fitting blouse that shapes my chest unbecomingly. My right breast is less than perky; it's maybe lopsided, maybe droopy, it's natural the way a breast is without padding or support. Bethany isn't looking at that breast though, she's looking at the left one that was there last week, but is now missing. That side of my chest appears almost concave the way the shirt falls on it.

Bethany is a little taken aback. She expected me to be modest about it. She expected me to look the same with clothes on because I would make an effort to appear normal. She's wrong. I want everyone to see what's happened. I want them to be torn between disgust and admiration.

Frank is the only one who doesn't pretend not to stare at my chest. He asks right away, "Are you going to get an implant?"

"I was thinking of just cutting the other one off."

Frank gives me an annoyed smirk while everyone else around me laughs uncomfortably and I offer a brave smile.

No one else says anything about it but I can imagine they are all talking about me. Every time I see anyone in conversation I imagine them saying things like "What do you think she looks like naked?" or "It's disgusting, I would have stuffed my bra" or "Have you ever fucked a chick with one tit?"

I see my boss on the phone and I can hear him in my head saying "She only has one breast. I don't think she should be working at the receptionist's desk. It's disgusting. I can't fire her though. We'll be sued."

He reluctantly makes eye contact with me later and then I'm sure that was his exact phone conversation.

At the end of the day Rachel pulls me aside. We have hardly ever talked and so I can't gauge her reaction to me but I assume she's going to privately confess what a role model I am.

"I thought you should know," She begins, "That everyone knows what happened."

"Knows what?"

That I have one breast? No shit, Sherlock.

"That you didn't have breast cancer," She tells me patiently.

This is news to me, and I don't believe it. She's assuming something because she's jealous of me and of all the attention I'm getting. She wants to appear selfless and can't stand that no matter what she does now, I'll always be seen as the martyr.

"Diane talked to your boyfriend – ex-boyfriend," She corrected herself quickly. "When you were first in the hospital and no one knew what had happened, she called your home and he picked up. He told her that he broke up with you and so you cut your breast off."

The jealous bitch. It figured she would make up some sort of crazy lie to bring me down to her level, as if that were possible. She wouldn't know what it was like to lose a breast, she hardly had any now. She wouldn't know what it was like to face death; she wishes her boring life involved something as exciting as that.

I wasn't going to stand around and let this woman accuse me of these vile things. I wasn't going to dignify her with a response. I grabbed the pen off the desk and plunged it into my right breast.

That self-satisfied smirk fell dead away from her malicious face.

"Now everyone is going to know how jealous you are of me. Everyone is going to know you want to take my other breast away."

She is paralyzed as I begin screaming but that just makes her look more guilty when I tell everyone she stabbed me.

I Love, Love, Love You

I love you, I love you, I love you.

I'm sure I do.

I must.

I have to.

Sometimes though,

I want to put my hand over your mouth to muffle your voice.

I want to clamp my hand down so hard that I can't even hear you whimper.

I want my nails to puncture your skin.

Make it bleed.

I want to feel your fragile bone break and burst under my palm.

I see you.

Beautiful,

Sweet,

Innocent.

But when I close my eyes I see you slick with blood.

Your whole body twisted and crushed to a pulp.

I want you.

I wanted you.

I want this to end.

I wasn't like this before you.

I wasn't disgusting,

Immoral,

Morbid.

My darling,

My baby,

My child.

I can't look at you.

I know I'll kill you.

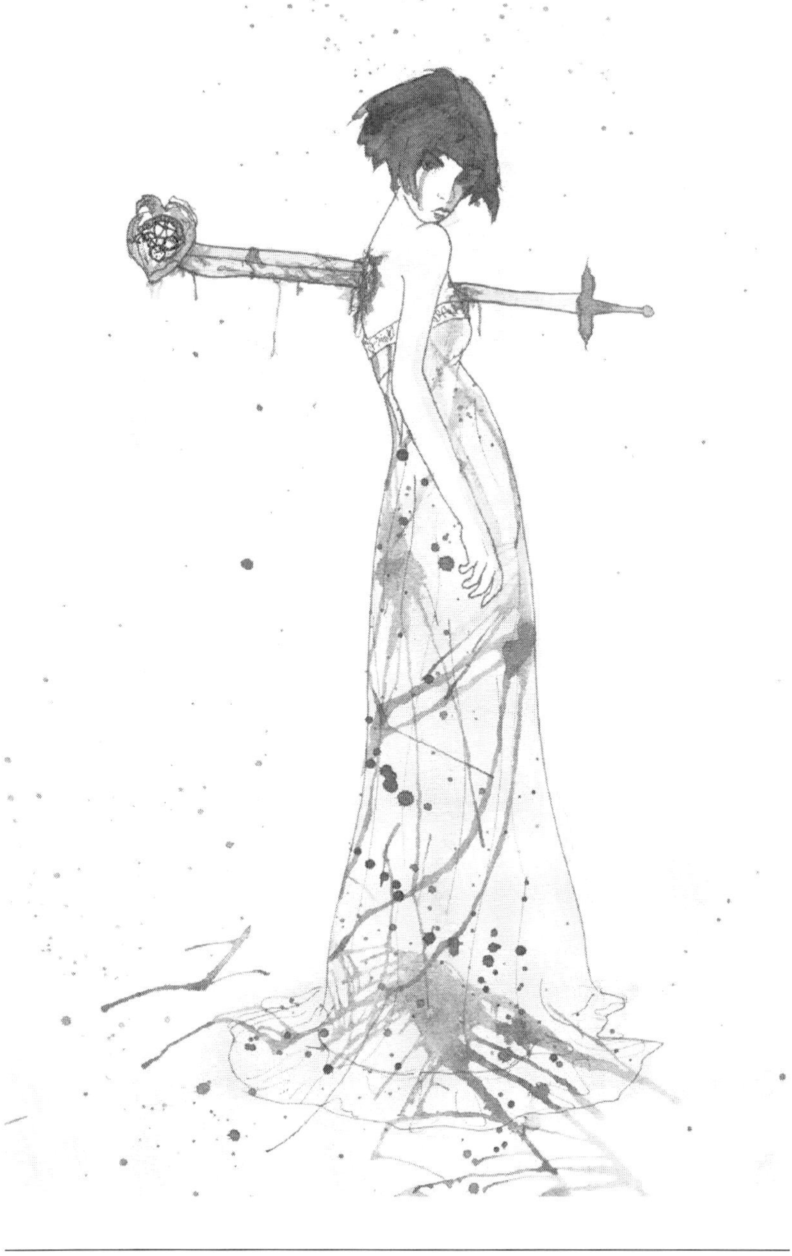

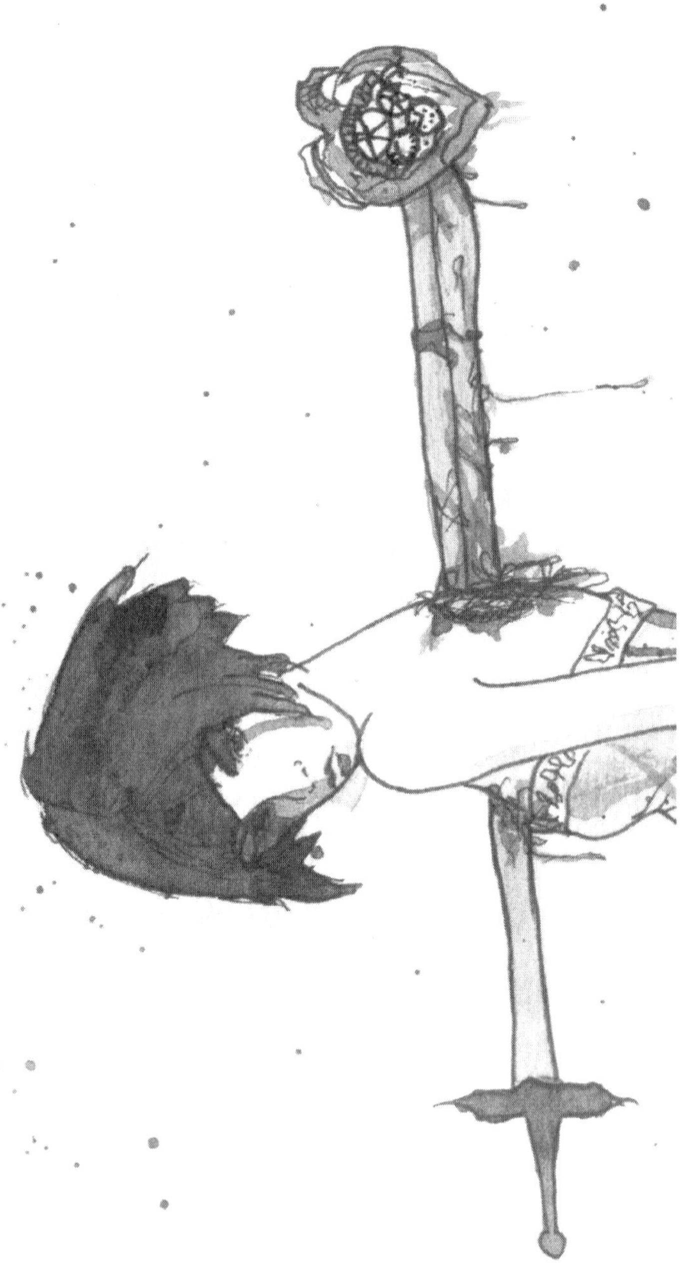

My Boyfriend

There are a lot of problems you don't consider the opposite sex having to deal with. Don't you just feel surprised when you see shows on men being beat by their wives? It's sort of weird at first and then it's just sad. What guy gets beat by his wife?

Anyway, my boyfriend has a problem I didn't think any guy had. He's bulimic. It seems like a cheerleader problem doesn't it? But no, my boyfriend has it and he's a college graduate and not girlie at all, not even a metrosexual. He binges and purges just like the girls you see on disorder documentaries (I've begun watching them since I've found out my boyfriend was one of them).

At first, to be totally honest, It was kind of funny. It's just funny, admit it. But then I got to thinking about what the repercussions might be. His teeth might fall out. His hair might fall out. He could have a heart attack...or something. He wouldn't be too good looking then.

But he might be even worse fat. When I think of him as fat I don't see the stocky version of him but the obese-covered-in-Cheetos-playing-DDR-with-the-controller-mode-all-Friday-night-in-his-room fat. I can't date that.

My only option is to dump him or wait and see what happens; see how this whole thing plays itself out.

I think I'll set a weight range for him. If he gets too big I'll drop notes like asking if he's "really going to eat all that?" when we go out for dinner. If he gets too thin I'll just cheat on him. I'm not sure how else to demean someone who's thin. It's like telling Jesus he isn't a people person.

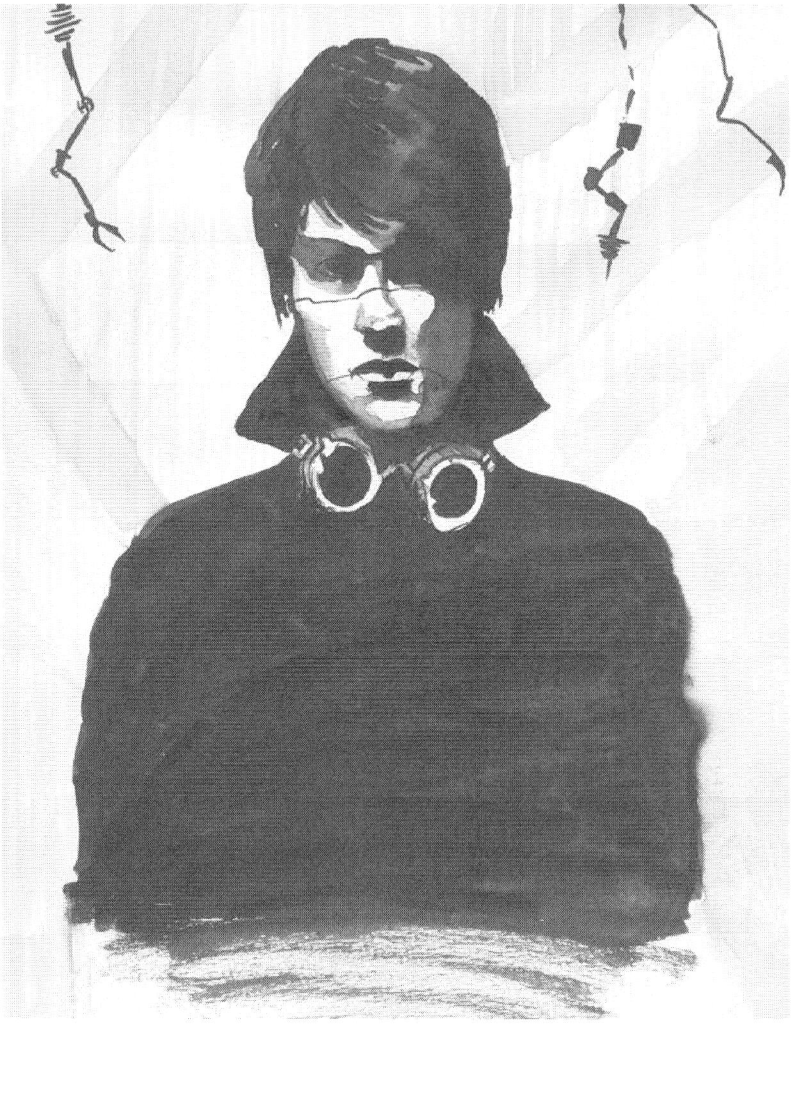

Super Hero

When I was young I wanted to be in some sort of chemical spill and become a super hero. Then I got older and realized that being saturated in toxic chemicals doesn't make you a super hero, it kills you.

And so, I'm drawing comics that take a stereotypical comic-like situation like that and follow it with the realistic outcome.

I know what you are thinking. A comic about a dude getting covered in chemicals and dying is going to be pretty short.

That's why I'm giving him cancer; it'll drag it out.

His arch nemesis is his girlfriend who stays with him out of obligation.

Fathers And Sons

I used to compare the size of my hands to my father's. His were so much bigger than mine, it amazed me. It amazed me more then his towering height or his girth, which I always assumed were what dads looked like, not that I would look like that too, when I was a grown man.

I guess it wasn't long into my life, as lives go, when it began. It was slowly at first. Things he would say when we were alone, or looks he would give me. Then it became physical. It was then that the size of his hands no longer amazed me, but terrified me. As did that trademark dad height and girth.

It went on for years and years – and everyone knew. How could they not? It had to have of been obvious. I tried to make it obvious. I know at least my mother saw the marks on me.

No one did anything though, so I didn't say a word either.

It was the cause for a lot of my problems, I guess. I was so introverted and aggressive. I wanted to think I had gotten over it though, that I had moved past it. I could hold down a job, I got married, I was normal like everyone else. I even had a child.

And watching my wife give birth was one of the best moments of my life.

No, it *was* the best.

I promised my son the moment that I held him in my arms that things would be different. Every other child in the hospital might go home with abusive or neglectful parents, but not him. He was going to have the most loving, attentive, and safest upbringing ever.

And I couldn't keep my promise.

It wasn't long into his life, as lives go, when I began. It was slowly at first. Things I would say when we were alone, or looks I would give him. Then it became physical. It was his size that terrified and excited me. My son's small and soft body.

It's been going on for years now, and no one knows. How can they? I've made sure it isn't obvious.

It's usually in the night I go to him. Sometimes he says it hurts, but sometimes he doesn't say a thing, and I know it doesn't hurt at all. Sometimes it feels good.

I know, because I've been there.

Mirror, mirror on the wall

MISSING
RACHEL'S PHONE NUMBER

My Best Friend

I'm terribly jealous of my best friend, but I can't tell her how I feel. She constantly tells me how beautiful and funny I am, but she has no idea how inept I am beside her.

She isn't a classic beauty, or a trendy beauty; she is an eternal beauty. No one can deny how lovely and angelic her face is. But, besides that, she has always been thin yet curvaceous: a body that you only see after airbrushing in magazines. Smooth and flawless skin. Long soft hair. She is everything I want to be. The one every girl envies and every boy covets.

I've never been thin, or even proportionate. I have never known a day when I could admire myself. Never even just my skin, my hair, my nails, or anything at all. I am the girl that disappears behind the others and struggles to find acceptance.

And even given all this, I feel for my best friend.

Perhaps because of her angelic beauty, or just because that's the way life is, her stepfather molests her. And because of that she doesn't comprehend boundaries. She devalues her body while at the same time concentrating all her energy into refining it, because it's the only thing she finds self worth in.

Still, I'm jealous. I would give anything to be her, to be molested. To be worth molesting.

What You Mean To Me

I've never really loved you. And if I honestly think about it, I never really even liked you either.

There comes a time in everyone's life when we just become too lonely. Your friends grow up and away from you; they become new people that have no connection to you. Your family becomes distant: some part of a life you hardly remember. Relationships become a case study of "history repeats itself" and you learn too late that it's because no one changes, including you.

You become too lonely to hold any high standards, and settle for not just someone, not someone below you, but someone who is also ready to settle. For you.

Think about it: isn't that how we were?

I'm not saying that we were wrong. Actually, if I could go back, I would have settled a lot sooner. I'm also not saying I regret I settled with you. A warm body is all the same to me, and it meant a lot when yours would hold mine.

Not to be sentimental or anything.

But your body isn't warm anymore and I find myself lonely again.

This is me trying to express my feelings for you. You understand how hard this is for me, right? I've never been the romantic sort. It's hard for me to say things like "You're important to me" or "I miss you." So, I've got to hope you know how much you mean to me when I tell you; I wish you hadn't died.

Online Predator

I watched "To Catch a Predator" for the first time the other night. I knew the concept of the show, was scandalized about it just like everyone else, and so I was shocked to feel myself relating to the predators.

It isn't that I've ever molested a child, or even propositioned one. I've never entertained thoughts or had urges. But, the chat logs were very familiar.

How old are you?

13?

Do you know what I'd like to do to you?

I'm going to bend you over and take you.

Hard.

I'll break you in two.

How would you like that, huh?

Tell me your address, I'll come over there right now and fuck you up.

I'll teach you how this is done.

These are the same things I've said over my head set while playing Halo3. I'm worried one of those kids might turn out to be a cop, but I can't help but pwn those n00bs.

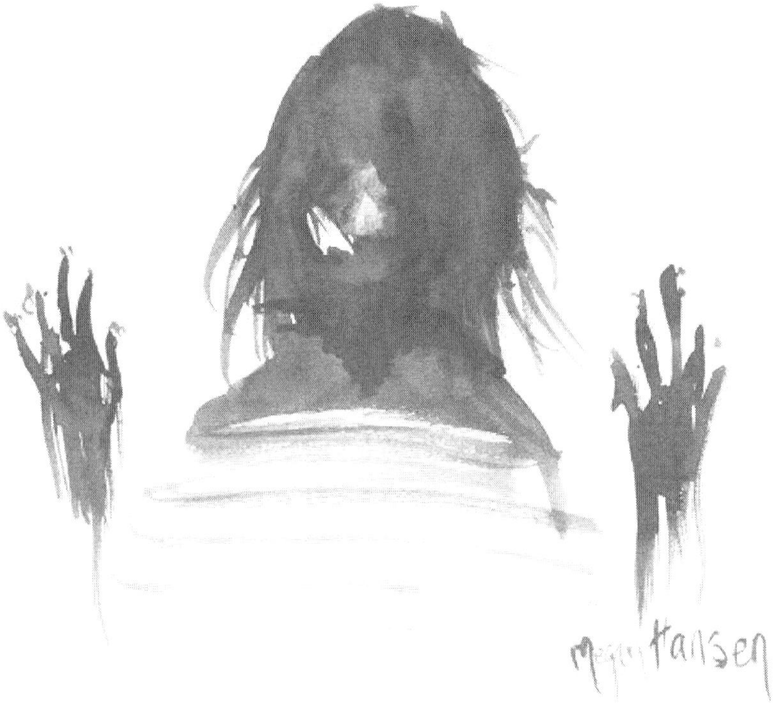
Megan Hansen

<u>Art</u>

There are so many criminal shows on TV now that people are afraid murderers are getting tips. They're probably right, but what they should really worry about are themselves being desensitized to the crimes.

Your run-of-the-mill murderer will still throw his pregnant wife down the stairs or shoot his neighbor over some petty quibble; it doesn't matter what's on TV. The true artists will always improve their craft and think outside the box. Hopefully the populace will appreciate the thought and effort put into it.

That's why I make sure to go into the clinics only on Wednesdays. That's when Tiffany works and each time I come in for an abortion she looks a little more disturbed.

She recognizes the originality and commitment I put into this.

Merry Christmas

It happened so fast.

I was driving late one night, returning home from a Christmas party, while my wife sat beside me in the passenger seat.

Everything was peaceful as the Christmas lights rushed passed us and the radio softly played carols.

Everything was perfect.

For once.

I hit that tree and the next thing I knew I was in the hospital.

It was so perfect.

So perfect.

Then I was informed that an accident had happened.

The one where her airbag deployed even though I silently begged it not to.

Now I'm paralyzed and my wife feels sorry for me.

Still, I feel like deep down she knows, and might be poisoning me.

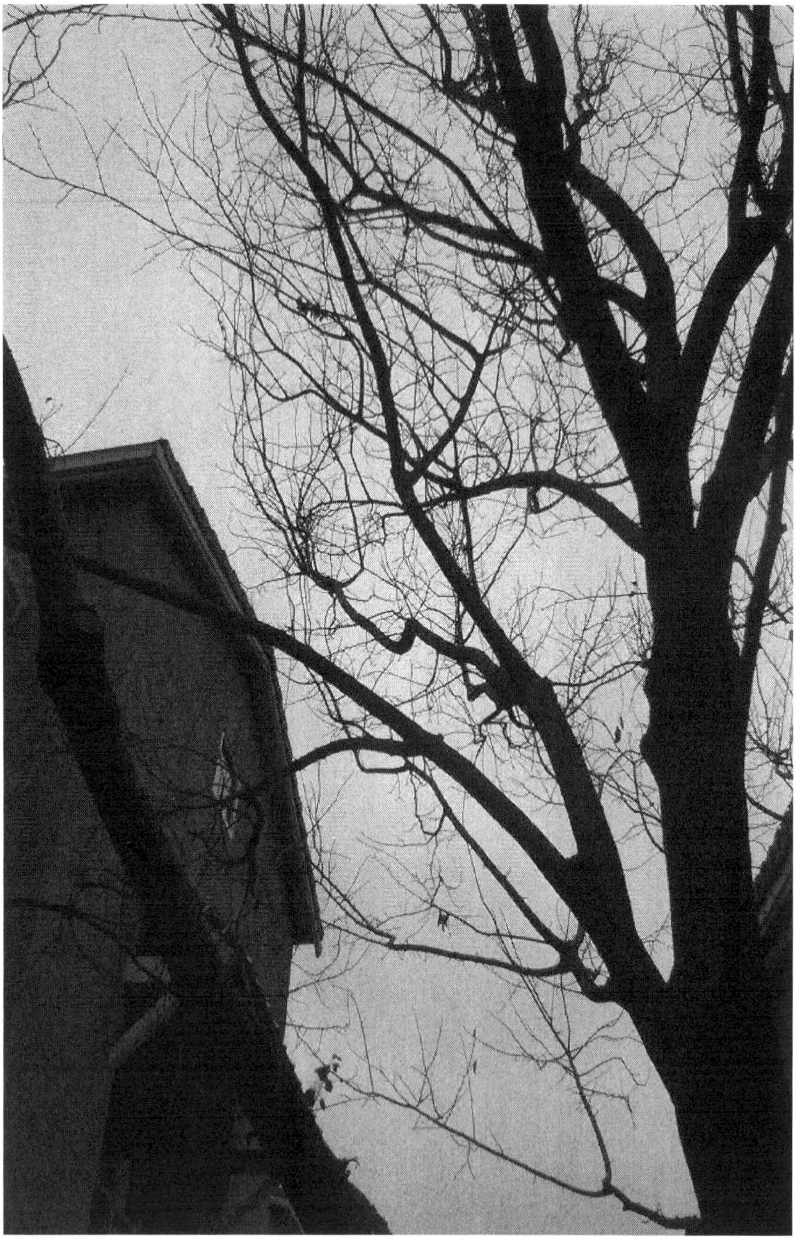

Waiting For Daddy

My older sister, Elizabeth, and I have to stay in our room while mommy meets her boyfriends.

Elizabeth keeps me company while we wait and she distracts me from the noise coming from outside our door. Sometimes it's too loud though, and that's when we listen to music with our headphones.

Mommy said it wasn't that she was trying to hide us from them, but them from us. She said that sometimes the boyfriends weren't good men, like our daddy had been. I never knew him because he left when I was a baby. Elizabeth tells me he and mommy used to fight a lot, and mommy says he'll come back to us one day.

Once she's done with her boyfriends.

Tonight she's done earlier than I thought she would be so I make sure to hug her extra tight so she knows how happy I am, and maybe next time she will be as quick as she was this time.

"Did you two have fun?" She asks us both but is looking only at me.

"Yeah, we played games."

"Good. That's good." She kisses me on the top of my head and smiles gently at Elizabeth who seems sad for some reason.

I think maybe she's happy we got let out early and is worried about next time. "How long do your boyfriends have to keep coming over, mommy?" I ask for the both of us.

My mommy gives me the gentle smile now and rubs her stomach. "I think it'll be very soon, but I can't take the test just yet."

Mommy promised us this was the last time she would need to make a baby. She thought so last time too, but changed her mind afterward. I think she's done now though; I think she looks like a princess.

She doesn't think so. She says she has to be just a bit more pretty for daddy, and then he'll want her back. She says if she can eat just another one of her babies she'll be young and pretty enough for him.

I hope she's not lying this time. I'd like to meet daddy.

I Love Animals

I love animals, I always have.

All kinds: cute or not, large or small, mammal or amphibian, indigenous or not, feral or not. I love them all. As a child, I wanted to run away to a zoo, be a veterinarian, live in Africa and patrol poachers. Most of all, I wanted a pet, but I couldn't have one. My mother was incredibly allergic. The best I got was a goldfish that I couldn't pet and who would forget who I was every three seconds. I tended to forget about him just as quickly.

For years, I had to get my fill of affection and loyalty only a pet could deliver at my friend's house until one day in the seventh grade when I was walking home from school. One of our neighbor's cats, Twinkie, had been hit by a car and lay–dead as a doornail–along the side of the road. He must have just been nicked because he didn't have any visible lacerations. He looked as if he would pop up at any moment to chase a bird or something. That was the only way I could rationalize to myself at that time why I began petting it.

Something in me found it macabre, but at the same time comforting. I could keep this cat and it wouldn't have to be left behind at a friend's house. It wouldn't shed all over the house. I could keep it stored away in my closet for just my own child-like pleasure.

So, I did.

I kept it in a suitcase in my closet and I even put it in the bed with me while I slept. It began decomposing pretty quickly though, and I hadn't been expecting that. I guess I should have, but it just didn't occur to me at the time. I blame public schools.

I dumped the body of Twinkie in the park and mourned my loss until I came across a second dead dog on the way back home. No collar, not too big to carry and hide, the lower half of his torso only partially torn away from the top, which was okay because my mother had been teaching me how to sew.

  I went through too many of these pets to count before I became an adult and got out on my own. I then tried living animals, but I had become too complacent with the dead ones. They never needed to be potty trained, walked, fed. My first living animal ended up deader than the ones I had been collecting before, so I kept to my old habits.

  You might suggest taxidermy, sure, I've tried that too. It just isn't the same. For one, they look alive and so it makes me quite sad to see them. I wonder what they were like, if they had a name or a family. It's depressing. Things that look vibrant and alive should be just that, alive. My dead pets didn't offer any false advertising like that. And besides, the pure delight and surprise of finding some nearly pristine road kill is invigorating. Christmas has nothing on it.

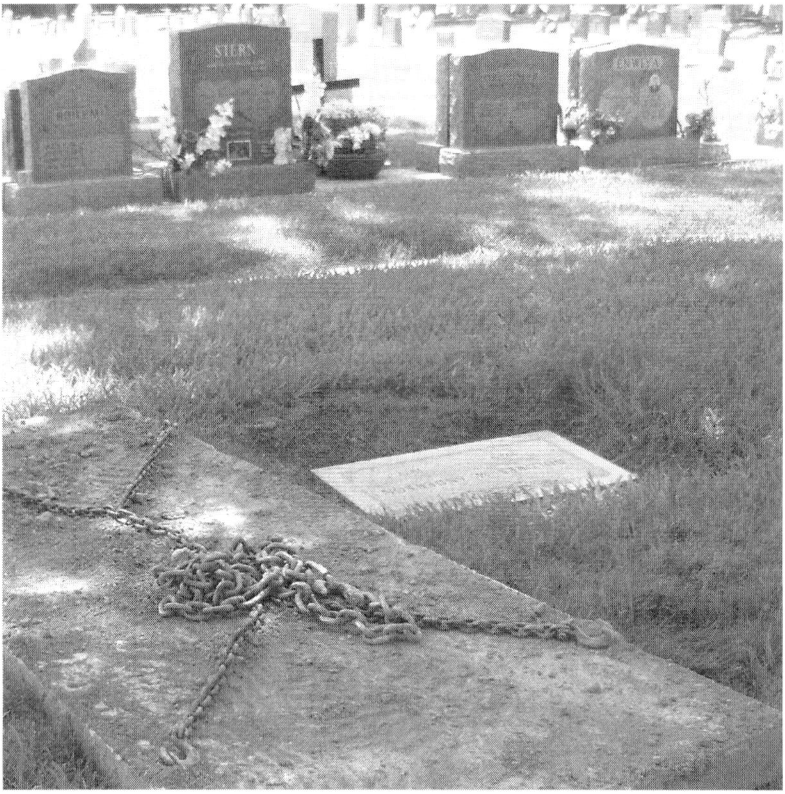
STERN

Backstreet Boys 2001 Black and Blue World Tour

It began the day a teenaged boy went into our high school and shot thirty-eight people: twenty-two of them died. Afterward, he shot himself in the head. Unfortunately for him, he didn't die immediately. He was in the ICU for forty seven hours before passing.

He was wearing a Backstreet Boys 2001 Black and Blue World Tour T-shirt at the time of the shooting. The media decided it was satirical and blamed the incident on Marilyn Manson anyway.

That night he visited me in a dream. He asked me if he made the news. Instead of answering him, I asked him why he didn't shoot me.

I don't know why I asked that, but in dreams you do a lot of things you don't understand.

He never answered my question.

That was last year, when I was a sophomore. I didn't dream of him again until a week ago.

He came to me while I was taking a test in my calculus class, suddenly appearing in the desk next to me. No one else in my dream seemed to notice him.

"Does anyone remember me?" he asked.

"No," I said quickly, not needing to think about it.

"Is anyone worried about dying anymore?"

"No," I answered just as quickly as before. After a moment I added, "I worry about it more and more each day."

He nodded thoughtfully, as if taking it into consideration.

When I woke up I remembered he was wearing the same Backstreet Boys T-Shirt he had on at the time of the shooting. I don't think it was satirical at all, I think he genuinely likes the band.

I Can Wait For You

The only time Robert had talked about his past was when he told Heather she could stay with them. It wasn't anything much, but he did it to make her feel comforted, and it worked.

"I've been on my own since I was about your age too."

"Really?" Heather asked.

He only nodded in response. There was a sort of kinsmanship between them then, but perhaps only Heather had felt it. Robert had never again related himself to her, or even once asked her how she had gotten where she was.

Something made her think he was trying to make things easier that way. Their pasts don't matter, they can coexist like normal people.

It wasn't that way for her though.

Deep down, she really wanted him to ask her what had happened, why she was in the position she was. Part of that was because she wanted understanding once all the facts were laid out, but also because she wanted to ask him about his past too.

Robert worked as a bouncer at some club Heather was too young to get into. Once she thought it would be a romantic idea if she went to work there too. Maybe she could be a waitress or a stripper. No matter how desperate you were for money though, or how rebellious you wanted to be, some women just weren't right for those jobs. As it was, she had gotten a job at a McDonalds.

When she looked at her life now, in the adventurous way rebellious young people do, it seemed like it was just her and Robert, but that wasn't true. Scott was with them too.

Scott wasn't like her or Robert. He didn't have a mysterious past none of them talked about. Scott had left his family to move to the city. When he didn't have enough money to live on anymore, Robert took him in as a roommate. Sometime after that was when Heather entered their lives.

Technically, she was the third wheel, but really, Scott was the outsider. He could always go back home. Most of the time, Heather wished he would.

There was a time when Heather was so sure she would wake up to Robert climbing into bed with her. He would say something about not being able to keep himself from her any longer, or he wouldn't say anything at all. He would brush the hair from her face and kiss her really softly. When they had sex he would be really gentle and tell her that he loved her.

Sometimes she would imagine this as she heard Scott with him through the wall. Most of the time it made her too angry to touch herself. Robert never said he loved him though, not that Heather could hear, and she made sure to listen carefully for it.

When she and Scott were alone, mostly at breakfast, he would ignore her. He seemed to think she wasn't worth his time but he was wrong. Scott couldn't be anything to Robert or her in the long run; he couldn't understand people like them. She saw that clearly, so Robert must have.

The best thing that could have happened was did, when Scott began turning yellow and vomiting. He had hepatitis C but Robert still wasn't done with him. It was frustrating at first but Heather's odds were better then, at least, than they had been. She could at least hope that it might kill him.

As soon as she was old enough, Heather would drink to Scott's health. Maybe he would join her.

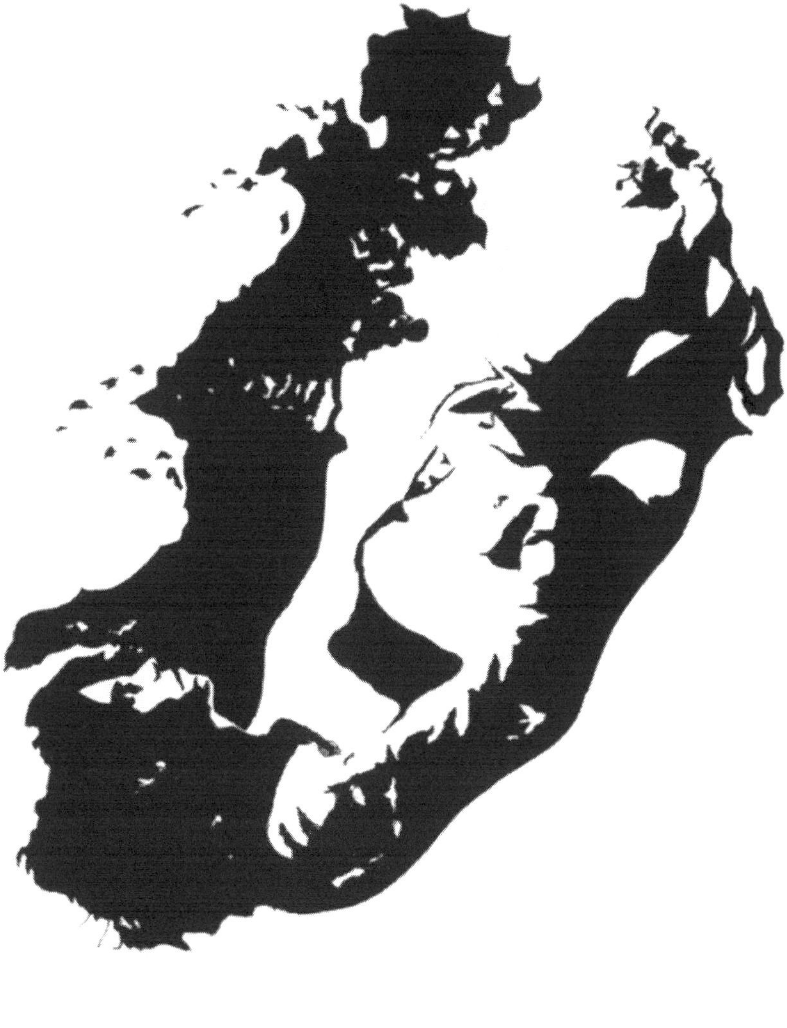

I Don't Like You

Have you ever met anyone you just liked right off the bat? Or heard someone talk about meeting someone who was just so delightful? There are people who are just so likable that we can't help but be drawn to them. People will often say to them, "Oh, I like you so much," or "Aren't you sweet? I love your company."

But, if there are people like that, then surely there are people out there that everyone just does NOT like. People that no one wants to be around or look at. People will say "I just didn't like him," or "There was just something about her I didn't like. I can't put my finger on it."

I'm one of those people.

I don't know when it happened, assuming I wasn't born this way, but as far back as I remember no one has liked me.

Not even my mother particularly cared for me. Not that she was abusive, but she really tried to avoid having much interaction with me. When we were alone and forced to talk the conversation would inevitably lag and she would say things like "Well, your sister is a dear, isn't she?"

I can't be certain, but I don't think I was breastfed either.

Though I've never acted out or have made a spectacle of myself teachers would always say "I've got my eye on you." As if I was up to something dubious. My test scores always came back low unless a TA had corrected them. That was, until the TA met me. It was a wonder I ever graduated at all.

Getting a job wasn't easy either. No one would call me in for a second interview, whether I was underqualified, overqualified, or adequately qualified. People will tell you anyone can get a job at a fast food restaurant, but that isn't true. Not if you are as unlikeable as I am. It took me a good long time before I was hired on at a Wendy's. It wasn't my dream job by any means but it WAS a job, so I was happy enough. I didn't take into account that my unlikeability would hinder me from keeping it though. It's not anything I did that got me fired, not at all.

In fact, it's what I didn't do, and that was serve people.

But I TRIED to serve people, really I did. No one wanted me to serve them though. A few people even had the gall to ask me "Can someone else take my order?" What could I say to that? I would go and find someone to take their order.

If I was physically or mentally disabled, the government would step in to help me care for myself, but there are no disability checks for people who are simply unlikeable. Though I assure you, it IS a disability. It is a liability. It is a... hindrance. So now I cannot support myself, have no one to help support me, and I cannot panhandle. No one gives unlikeable bums spare change.

As if all this wasn't bad enough, I must admit I don't much care for myself either. It isn't self-loathing or self-pity, no... There is just something about me I don't like; I can't put my finger on it. You might be saying, "Well, why don't you kill yourself then?" But I am a religious person and believe in an afterlife. I'm not looking forward to spending an eternity with myself.

Would you want to spend that much time with me?

I didn't think so.

Marine Biology

Hello everyone.

Thank you for having me in your class today, and thank you to Mrs. More for asking me to come speak to you all. I know some of the other parents have already come in and a fair share of them have more interesting than I do jobs, but I hope I can be a little bit entertaining, as well as informative.

Well, as some of you know, I'm Anthony's father. I'm a marine biologist and what that is, is a scientist that studies the animals in the ocean. I became interested in this field when I was about your age. See, my father was a fisherman and I would see numerous species of fish and I became fascinated by these alien creatures.

Picture a fish in your mind. Not the cartoon type, not the Nemo type. Not the fish sticks type either. Picture a real fish. Have any of you seen a real fish before? Here, pass these around...They are photos of different species of fish and octopi; I thought these would be the ones you might most readily associate with ocean life. You may wonder why I'm not suggesting sharks or dolphins, as you all surely have a better, more accurate, representation of them in your imagination. Well, that's just my point. There are innumerable other creatures and life forms in the ocean, more then science even knows of now. We discover more all the time, sometimes confounding the leaders in my field. Maybe one day we'll discover a mermaid. Maybe you'll grow up to be the marine biologist who does just that.

Now that you have a better idea of these funny-looking creatures and the mysteriousness of the ocean, consider what life in the ocean is like. There is life, death, evolution, eating, sleeping. Just like here on land. Your lives are a lot like the ones of sea creatures. Have you heard of schools of fish? Well, those schools are essentially what this classroom is. We, like fish, learn from life experiences and as the fish learn from their survival and natural instincts, we put ourselves in school to experience a text book education. We can afford to do this because our lives are longer, we're more highly evolved, and our impact on the world is greater than that of a fish's.

Have any of you been molested? I see a few hands there. Did you know that dolphins are the only animal on Earth besides humans to gang rape? It's true. They are very intelligent, more so than monkeys, and you've seen some of those speak in sign language, right? In fact, dolphins are more like us than you might think. Their flippers have almost the exact same bone structure as your hand.

Another interesting fact you can impress your friends with is that sharks don't sleep. They alternate between active and inactive states. As humans we need at least seven hours sleep. Another difference, among many, is that sharks have no bones. They have cartilage. Feel your nose, see how it can move but it's still firm? That's cartilage. It's what makes the sharks naturally buoyant. Humans are weighed down by 206 bones (in an adult) and the highest rate of drowning instances is in children. A phenomenon known as "dry drowning" takes the lives of many children each year, maybe you've heard it on the news? You can get water in your lungs while swimming and it will drown you internally even hours after you've left the water. You'll never see it coming.

My time is about up here. I want to thank you again for letting me visit your class. I hope I didn't embarrass you, Anthony. I know my science talk can be a bit boring sometimes. I'll see you when you come home – oh, and we'll have to talk about you raising your hand earlier. I've explained to you what would happen if you ever told anyone.

You'll Care About Me.

People who hurt themselves are doing it for others. No one really wants to be in pain; it's to get another's attention in some way. Most of these people put themselves through some masochistic self mutilation if they are desperate for attention. Maybe I'm being naive because I've never wanted to do something so theatric as stick a knife in my wrist, but it doesn't make sense to me.

I saw a girl on TV once who cut herself. She said it was like a release. When she cut herself, she could watch the blood slowly pour from her, and with it went her problems, for the time being. But, I've cut myself before, always by accident, and it never gave me any sort of release, only panic. Another young girl said she would hurt herself to feel pain. Life had become numb to her, and she would do it to feel something again.

Sure, people will treat you better if they know you are doing such things, but these girls kept it secret. They seemed to wait until the situation was so far along that the reaction was enormous. If they weren't doing it for others, why would they admit it all in the end? It's all for attention.

I don't want that surge of attention. I want people around me to love me and pay attention to me continually. It's what everyone wants, if they are being honest with themselves. Sometimes that's hard to get, that's why it's so valuable. If everyone loved and supported everyone else we wouldn't have people like those young cutter girls on TV all the time.

The attention they get is all wrong anyway. It's not fulfilling at all. Their friends and family give them panicked and pitiful reactions, but these things can't ever last long. Even if these girls keep at it, their loved ones will become tired and drained, and then eventually distance themselves. The best kind of attention was the attentive kind. You need for others to always feel the need to stay close to you or keep in constant contact. Be that out of protection for you or themselves.

I used to do lots of things to get attention from others. When I was young, I would cry and throw things until my mom would give me the attention I was looking for. When I was older I used to tell elaborate lies to my friends, trying to top theirs. Shortly thereafter I began to overtake their conquests, outdo them in anything they were interested in or sleeping with.

Life is different now, things aren't so simple. The outlets I had before didn't work as well in the adult world I had found myself in. I can readjust though. I have always found ways to make people care about me. I can do that again. It may take some time, but you can't rush things that are worth so much to you.

I keep telling myself that as I wait the necessary thirty seconds. The swab jammed between my cheek and gums is uncomfortable and sort of gratifying. Even though I still have a bit of waiting to do, I'm used to it. This is my fifth try.

When the time is up I hand the swab over and it gets stuck in the tiny tube, the end broken off, then closed inside with a little lid. It's going off to be tested, and with it goes my hopes.

Please, this time it has to work.

Please, this time come back positive.

Sometimes I think I understand Everything. Then I regain Consciousness. Everything

I would rather be Ashes than Dust. I would rather that My spark Burn out in a brilliant

I Want To Be Black

Sometimes I wish I were black.

Sometimes I turn off the lights and look at myself in the mirror, trying to see what I might look like. That doesn't really work, so I tried Photoshopping a picture of myself...But it came out looking sort of racist.

I know that it isn't always easy to be a minority. People won't look at you the same as if you're white. Sometimes they won't look at you at all. Sometimes too much. People will have preconceived notions about you. *She's violent. She's uneducated. She's into Jay Z.* I know it isn't easy to be black, and it would take some adjustment for someone as white as me to get used to the cultural differences and prejudges. I could do it though, if it were possible. I want it bad enough.

I think I might even be a better black woman than others I've seen. I wouldn't mimic white people. I would use whatever dialect that was most common in whatever area I resided in. If words have to be pronounced as always ending in vowels, so be it. If I have to use some genuinely offensive racial slurs in companionable ways, I can manage that. It doesn't make one uneducated. The English language is ever evolving, that's the reason it's still around. Why hinder the growth of fluidity of a language when the alternative is to let it die, as Latin had?

I wouldn't envy white women either; lighter skin isn't more beautiful, it's just another shade of black. I would prefer to have the darkest skin possible. Tyra Banks would call it dark chocolate, and when she says it, it sounds so enviable. I want Tyra Banks to look at me as if we're some sort of sworn sisters due to our common race and tell me in a sexy voice that I'm "dark chocolate."

I would embrace my heritage. Maybe I would wear African style clothes, and change my name to something regal sounding. Or I might just change it to LaQuisha, as to not sound uppity. How do people celebrate Martin Luther King Day? I'll find out. I'll go to rallies, or read some of his speeches aloud in parks. I would celebrate Kwanza and berate anyone who said the holiday was a joke.

I want to be black so badly.

No one understands why. My parents have even gotten angry, saying I should be proud of my heritage. They showed me old photos of my great-great-whatever on Ellis Island. They showed me photos of Ireland, and told me about the so called proud history of our ancestors. When I was unresponsive they threw out all my rap CDs, Ebony magazines, and Beyonce posters.

It didn't work. I'm not impressed, and it doesn't change my mind.

They don't and can't understand. Those I've told my reasonings to don't believe me either. They think I'm being irrational and trauma has me misguided. That I'm trying to project my fear outward, but that isn't true. The fear is coiled up inside my body tightly, no part of it can escape.

Sometimes I wish I were black.

That way, my aversion to white people would be easily explained.

And that way, I might be empowered and overcome my fear of them.

"Years of oppression and segregation! You can't hold me down any longer!"

But I'm white.

And so it's hard to explain why I can't stand being around white men.

No one treats me the same after I tell them that all the men who raped me were white.

Please Come

Her voice came through the line softly but I knew it wasn't my reception that was causing it. She was speaking in a low tone, ending all her sentences in a strain that snaked down into my chest and pulled on my heart.

"Please come, hurry," She begged.

"I'll be right there," I assured.

As I rushed there, all I could hear was her voice.

He got really drunk.

He was so angry.

He left me here.

All I could see was her face.

Pinched brow.

Tear-welled eyes.

Desperate, pleading, look.

As soon as I got there, all I found was that I had been wrong.

"Come have a drink with me. Don't look like that, come on. If I had just asked you to come meet me, would you have?"

Clever smile.

Laughing eyes.

Intimate hands.

"No, I wouldn't have come," I admitted.

"Then I had no choice but to lie to you, didn't I?" She asked, patting the stool next to her. "I know I can rely on you; you are such a good guy."

She rested her head on my shoulder and I could smell the alcohol wafting from her mouth into my nose. Not all together off putting, much to my chagrin, and mixed with the smell of her natural mouth. I could almost taste her on that scent.

"You are so funny," She told me. "You think I would let him touch me?" She laughed. "You wish he would, don't you?" Then she quickly jabbed me in the ribs and said "I'm joking."

She may be joking, but it's true. I may have felt worried or scared, but more then anything, I was so glad. I was so relieved to know he was a drunk, to know he hit her, to know she had called me to come to her rescue.

"Why do you always call me?" I asked, finding I said it so softly it was as if my voice was resisting me.

"Because you always come."

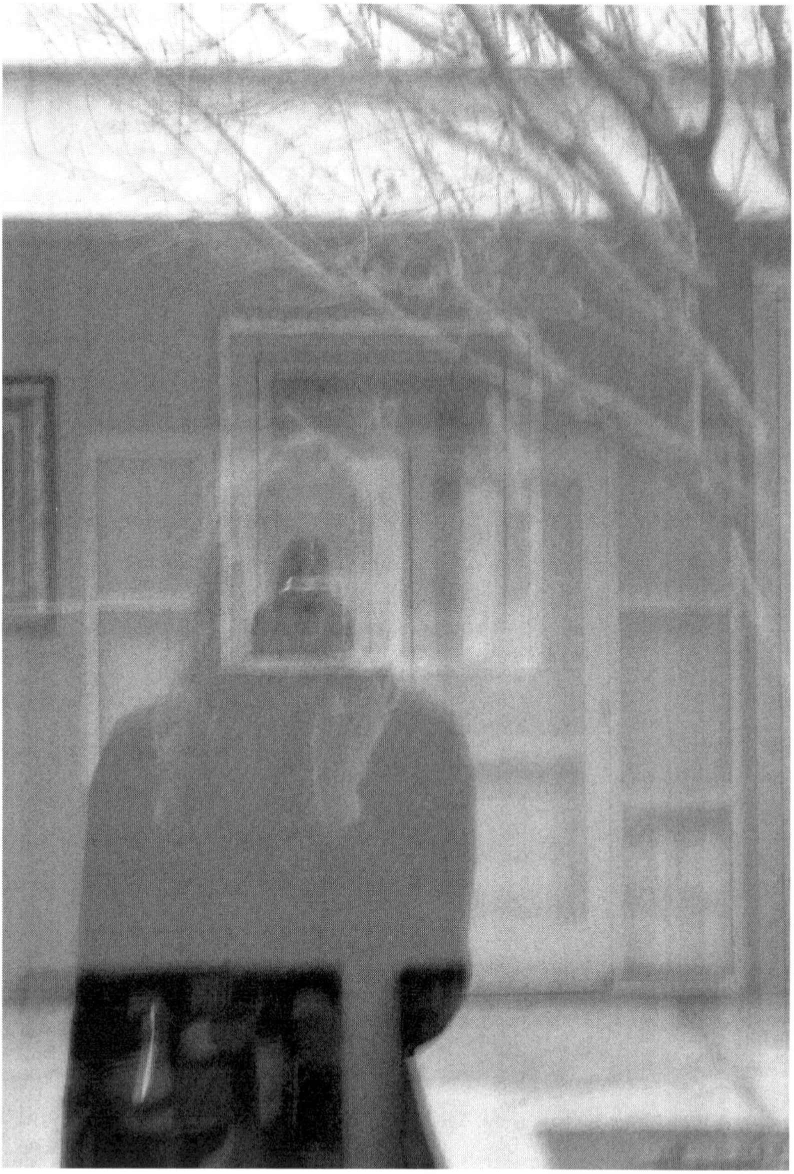

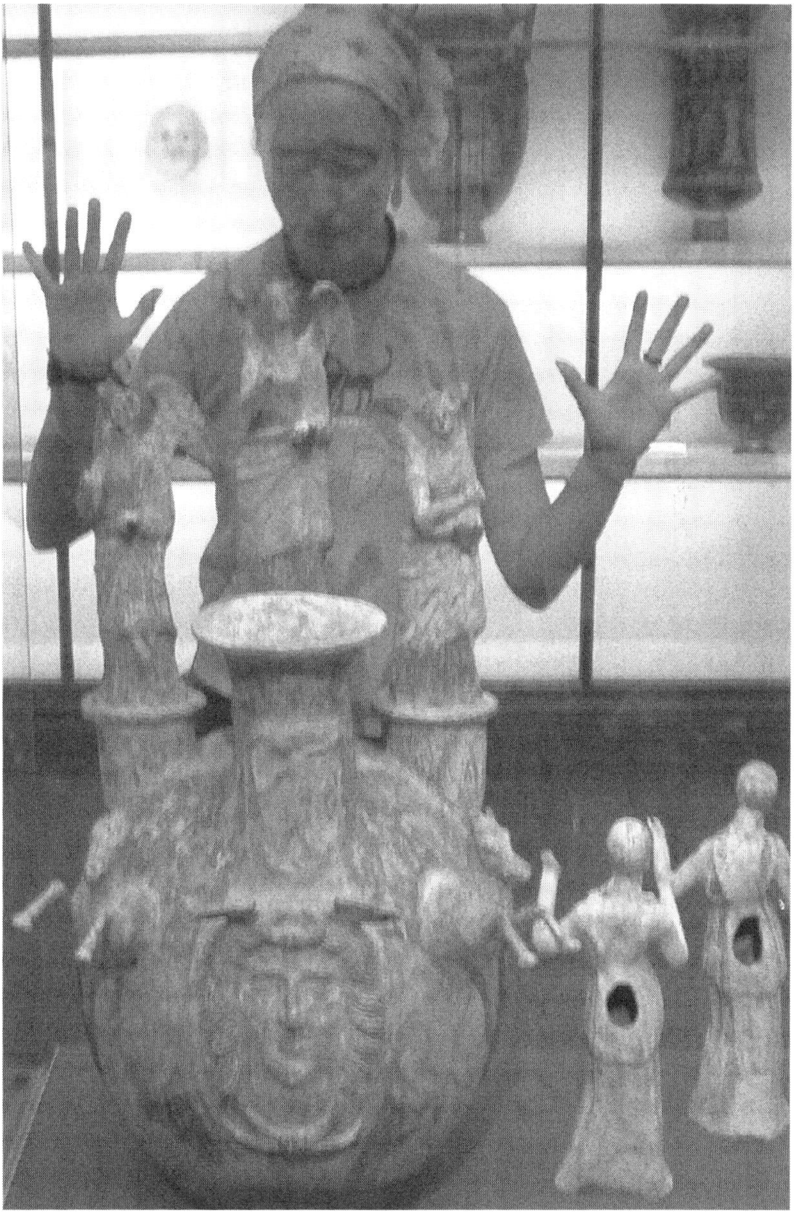

Feminism

For my final in Women's Studies I have decided to write an essay on how the feminist movement has given me a better life in modern America. I would like to begin by sharing that this subject is close to my heart as I am a strong independent woman whose respectability and intelligence wouldn't have been recognized if it weren't for my foremothers. I am also grateful to my father who has paid for my tuition through five changes of my major and two times on academic probation. Also, thank you Mr. Albion for letting me make up this final after I was out last week because of my period. I have super bad cramps and you were the only teacher to not be a dick about it.

For as long as humans have been evolved enough to form social structures a women's place has been below that of a man (besides the pagan traditions which recognized the sacredness of a woman's body and those matriarchal societies that prove to be less violent and more spiritual; those aren't as important because our protestant roots say so). Women have been seen as property and as faceless wombs, denied literacy or any chance at discovering any aptitude in a professional or even artistic field.

Christine de Pizan (1363-1434) is seen as the first feminist of the western world and is credited with being the first woman writer recognized for her talent. Even then, we have a classic and wildly popular novel such as *Frankenstein* (1818) that was written by a adept female writer, Mary Wollstonecraft Shelley, who had to publish her novel anonymously. It wasn't until 1831, during it's second publishing, was she credited with the work. Since then, women have come a long way and we have a plethora of, not just female writers, but material written by women for women. Romance novels are a multimillion dollar business. Even in this economic climate, Harlequin saw a $3 million gain in the last quarter of 2008. *Glamour*, *Vanity Fair*, *Cosmopolitan*, and *In Style* are just a few of the best-selling magazines. These publications lift up and empower women to be self-sufficient and cutting edge in the twenty first century and beyond. Woman are becoming more self motivated and informed of hygiene with articles such as "Wake Up With Sexy Hair", they are being empowered to take charge in relationships with innumerable and almost indistinguishable articles such as "Sex He Craves: We Help You Discover His Most Dirty-licious Fantasies - So You Can Deliver On The Naughty Goods", learning to be forward thinking and planners with "Why Men Cheat In August".

Even men's magazines have begun to elevate the image of women in such publications as *Maxim* where each issue is filled with sexy modern women. No longer are women chained to an oven, forced to wear wrist- and ankle-length dresses. Now, we are allowed to wear what we choose, what can arguably be the constant visual reminder of how far we've come and what women now represent. Tube tops, low rider jeans, thongs: these things no longer have a dirty or even low class connotation, they are simply popular styles of dress for women. We aren't sexual objects, but sexual beings who can express ourselves without labeling ourselves. This progression has even reached our children with infant and toddler versions of the same tube tops, low rider jeans, and smaller diapers to accommodate these garments.

Women are so prominent in the media in this modern age that we have limitless role models for ourselves and our children. Groundbreaking work such as *The Feminine Mystique* written by Betty Friedan and feminist icons such as Shirley Chisholm, Gloria Steinem, Geraldine Ferraro, and Robin Morgan were good enough for our mother's generation, but we have a culture that is now saturated with iconic women. You cannot turn on a television without being inundated with images of bold and alluring women, confirming the undeniable proof of woman's sexuality being a necessity in modern capitalism: validating our worth with every purchase from Carl's Jr., AX Body Spray, and donation to PETA. A modern-day feminist icon, Tyra Banks, is not only a pillar of entrepreneurial excellence – what with her years of modeling, producing and starring on a popular reality show on modeling, producing a reality show about modeling, and producing and hosting a talk show that primarily features modeling – but she has dedicated her life to encouraging women to accept themselves and find their own self-worth, and by that she concentrates solely on encouraging women to accept their bodies and find their self worth in the acceptance of said bodies.

We stand on the shoulders of those who have come before us and demanded their rightful place in this world. I feel a great weight as a woman to live up to the responsibility I've been given. To be a great daughter, mother, baby-momma, and the sexiest most sexually empowered girl at the all night kegers. This semester has born in me the flame of hope to one day become a leader in the modern feminist movement. I can and will be the force that blows new life into it, giving a face and name to associate with instead of those women now who's names I don't know because they weren't listed on Wikipedia.

Let's Part

Most people would say they have a fear of commitment, not of breaking it. But that's my problem. I can't bear to hurt others. I don't want to be the one to cause anyone pain, in any form. Above all, I don't want to hurt my wife.

She and I met in high school, a very important time in anyone's life, hormonally speaking, and we've been together ever since. She has been there for me at all the influential points in my life. My graduation from high school and then college, our marriage, the birth of our children, the death of my parents, and so on. My wife is a pillar of strength, integrity, and companionship. And I just don't love her anymore.

It isn't anything she's done. It isn't anything she hasn't done either. I just want to have a life away from her. I want a chance to see what type of person I can be on my own, because I've never been an individual. I've always been a son, and then her husband. There is no I, there is only us.

I cannot tell her this though, she wouldn't understand, and it would only hurt her. I wish there were another way to part from her, but I can't think of one.

My psychologist says it's time to start making the transition and so I'll have to tell her soon. I hope she'll be unable to stomach me anymore and leave quickly. I don't want to cause either of us pain.

If getting a sex change doesn't make her leave me, I don't know what will.

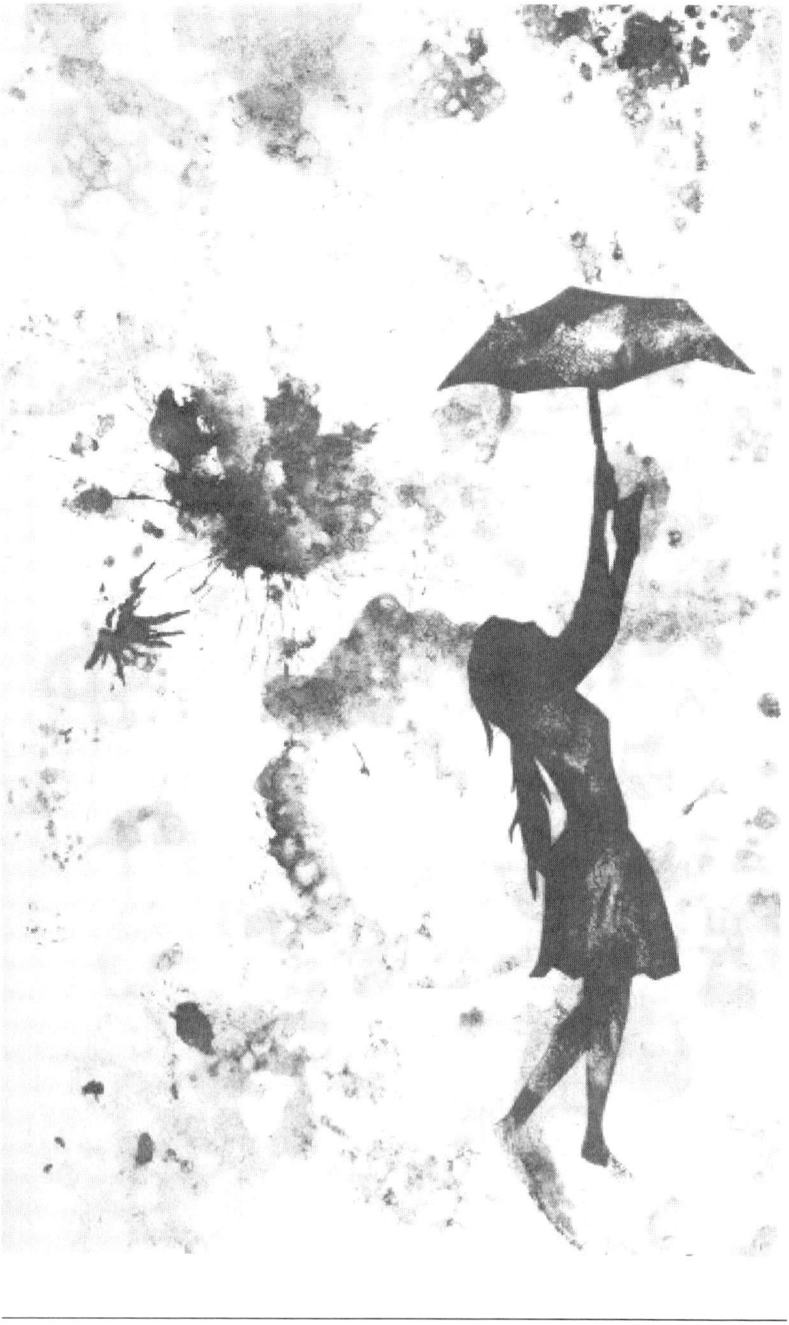

Karma

I always thought of myself as a strong and secure woman, but I must admit, you found a way to hurt me.

Never would I have thought you could have had such a deep effect on me, but you did. That must be because I was in love with you; I'm brave enough now to tell you that. I was more in love with you than I was with anyone before.

I won't let you blame me for what happened though, because I couldn't say I loved you at the time, or some such nonsense. If you were suffering from lack of love, you could have left me. You didn't have to cheat on me.

That was a total misuse of my heart and my time and my devotion to you. You wasted all of those gifts I gave you.

I wanted to find some way to make you pay, but I knew there was nothing I could do to you that would equate to the pain you caused me.

Then I found out your infidelity caused that woman's pregnancy. And the child had down syndrome.

Enjoy your retarded baby; you should call him Karma.

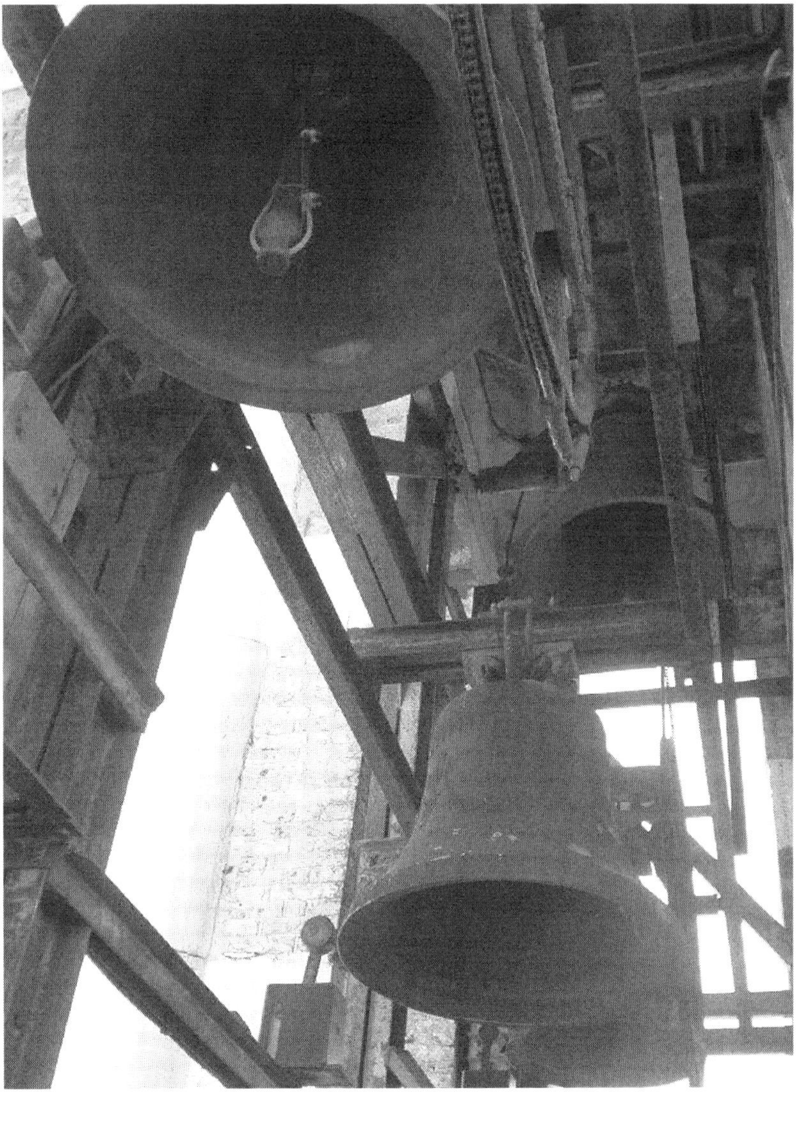

My Father

Most kids see their parents as unflawed authority, and then puberty comes and they see them as foolish dictators. I can't say my experience was much different, but it wasn't long after the puberty stage began that I saw my father in a whole new light. I think it's supposed to be around your twenties and thirties that you understand that your parents are simply human. Flawed, but doing what they can to live the best they can. I was only a freshmen in high school when I realized my parents were more than flawed.

I don't think my father had any intentions of letting any of his children, or anyone else for that matter, know about his childhood. The reason he had decided to "come clean," as it were, is because he agreed to give his testimony at a trial. It's not something I entirely understood at the time, I hadn't ever been to a courtroom or seen much of one on TV. I didn't go to the trial myself, but I heard my family talking about it and even people in town would bring it up, though usually not to me.

The testimony my father gave was a quick history and then a retelling of one night in particular. My grandmother, that I hadn't ever met, would service men in her home at night throughout my father's childhood until he was nearly thirteen, and then she died. The night she died was the night my father had to retell to the court.

A john had come home with her and my father hadn't seen either of them enter because he was already in bed. He was asleep through most of the man's visit but woke up to the commotion of the man raping and beating his mother. My father didn't move from his bed, but waited for the noise to settle down. Eventually it did and the man entered his room, and proceeded to rape him as well.

The man hadn't killed my grandmother. She apparently was taking drugs while her rapist was in her son's room and had (unintentionally?) killed herself. My father contacted the police in the morning when he found his mother's body but didn't tell them he had even seen the john. Apparently he was too ashamed and mortified to admit it at the time. I can understand how he felt, because that's the same way I felt when I heard the story.

He had wanted to tell us, his family, before he went to court. Explain it to us in his own words so we would understand. I guess that was his intention. I would rather he didn't tell us at all. After he finished the story there was silence and my mother patted his leg and told us how proud she was of him to be so honest. How brave he was to come forward and make sure this man couldn't hurt anyone else. He was a hero.

If he had kept it a secret that long, why would he tell us all now? It's not that I didn't feel for my father, it was a terrible thing to have to go through, I'm sure, but what about us? His children. Why burden us with this? Did he think I would be able to look at him after hearing this? See anything but a young version of himself being raped by some faceless visage of nightmares?

I deserved to have a father to loathe throughout my teenage years and then to turn to for leadership in my adulthood. What I have now is a rape victim for a father and a sympathetic but uncomfortable mother. What I have now are friends who wanted to know the details of the story and make me feel like an outcast. Their parents had never gotten raped, but who's to say that was true? I hadn't known my father had been either. I like to suggest that to them. Often.

As best I could, I tried to not let my uncomfortable feelings toward my father show, but that's hard to do. He's my father and I live with him, see him every day. For the longest time I thought I had done a good job though.

It was maybe a year after the trial had ended, and life had become more or less normal again, my father and I were alone in the car. He suddenly asked me "Do you love me?" Not demanding or hesitant like he was afraid of the answer, just curious.

"Yes," I said simply, but awkwardly, because I then realized I hadn't said that I had in quite some time.

"I love you too," He said in some sort of masked way. At the time I couldn't decipher his hidden meaning and as years passed my memory distorted the tone so even now, older and wiser, I can't tell what he meant.

My father never again asked me if I loved him, and I never again told him I did. I'm sure I do though. it's just hard to love someone you know too much about, and knowing about the night of my grandmother's death was more then I ever wanted to know about him.

Addiction

They say to quit smoking, you have to substitute the addiction. Something that keeps your hands busy.

That didn't work for me though. Unlike smoking, you can only masturbate in public for so long before someone calls the police.

Now I know how those breastfeeding mothers feel.

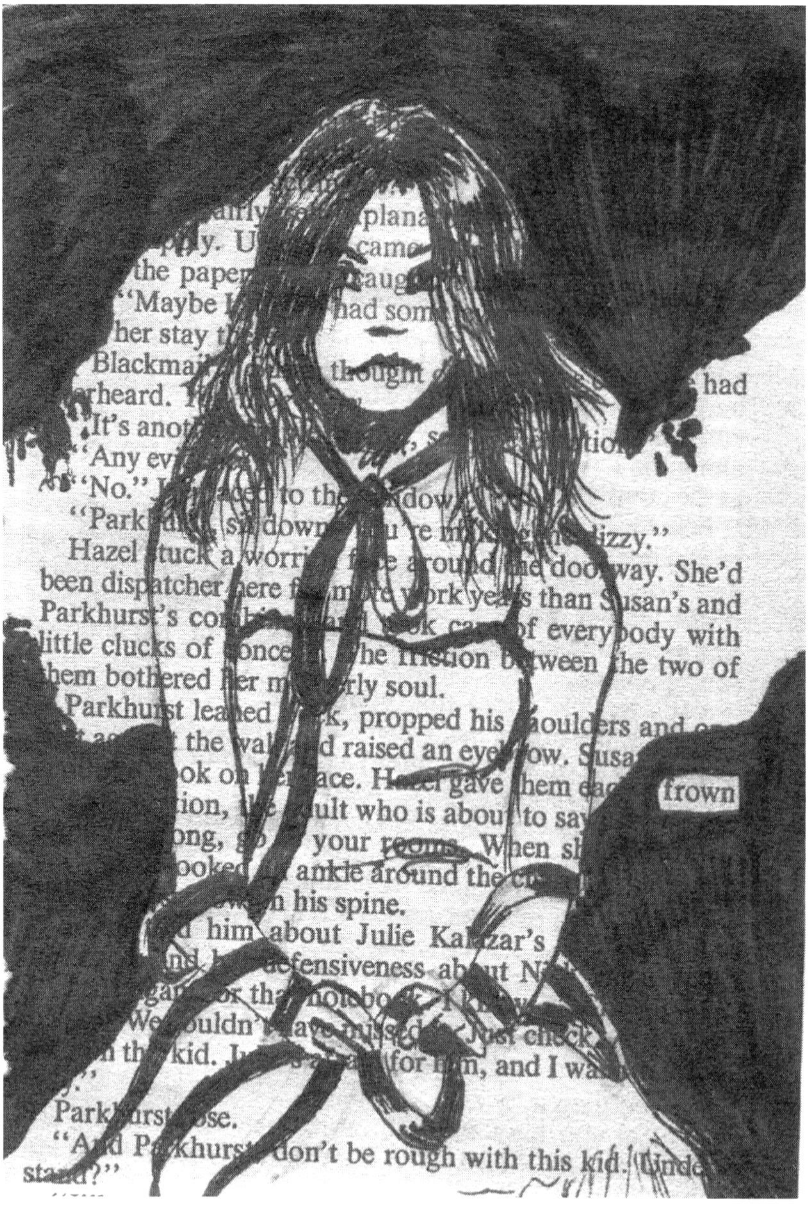
frown

With Time

You can't ignore things and expect them to go away. Everyone hears that throughout their life. It's one of the main reasons women go in for pap smears, or breast exams, and men go in for prostate exams. Pretending you don't have a problem, or not checking to find one, doesn't make you healthy. I can only hope this doesn't apply for things that aren't physical.

It's hard to stare something in the face that is so horrifying that it will change your life forever. You may judge someone for not stepping up and doing the right thing in those situations, but unless you are there, you can't know what it's like. We're all just human; we can't all be expected to be heroes.

Just like everyone else, I do what I can to live. Hand to mouth. Day to day. I would like to say I always did the right thing, but I can't. I can say I've always done what I thought was right at the time though. I can't help it if some of those things turned out to be the worst possible decisions.

I know now I shouldn't have brought that man into my house, my bed. I know I shouldn't have allowed him alone with my daughter. I know I should have believed her when she said he touched her. I know I shouldn't have felt jealous.

Knowing these things doesn't change the past, but I hope time might. I hope that with time she will forget. I hope with time I will forget. I hope with time I can ignore her crying in the night, the sounds of her vomiting in her closet, the cuts along her forearms and stomach.

BFF
(Beach Front Funeral)

When someone gets hit by a car, everyone calls 911 then the body is covered and taken away.

When a whale washes up on shore everyone gathers to watch it die.

And when I have funeral flowers delivered to the beach, everyone looks at me as if *I'm* weird.

No One Even Notices

The first time I heard about the pedophile was when I was heading to work. I had stopped just outside the apartment complex's gate, to retie my shoe, as some of the older women walked inside.

"There is a child molester in the building now," one said so suddenly, it startled me.

"You aren't serious, are you? Where does he live?"

"30B."

I quickly tried to recall if that was even near my place. It was.

Whatever else they might have said, I couldn't hear. They were now out of earshot.

The next time I heard anything about it was in the elevator, trying to reach my level.

"My wife is too worried to bring our grandchildren over." This time it was an older man.

"There really isn't anywhere but the park for our kids to play, but we've made sure to have someone there to watch them when they do," said a younger man.

"I can't believe what this world is coming to. Any man who would do that to a child should be killed."

They both agreed.

Not that I didn't hear more people talk, but mostly I could see people's reactions. Any time an unfamiliar man was on the property, the children stayed close to their parents, and the parents kept a close eye on them. It wasn't obsessive, but it also wouldn't last. People always become complacent.

It didn't bother me, I could wait. Everyone assumed the pedophile was a man, but I'm only a young woman. No one even notices me.

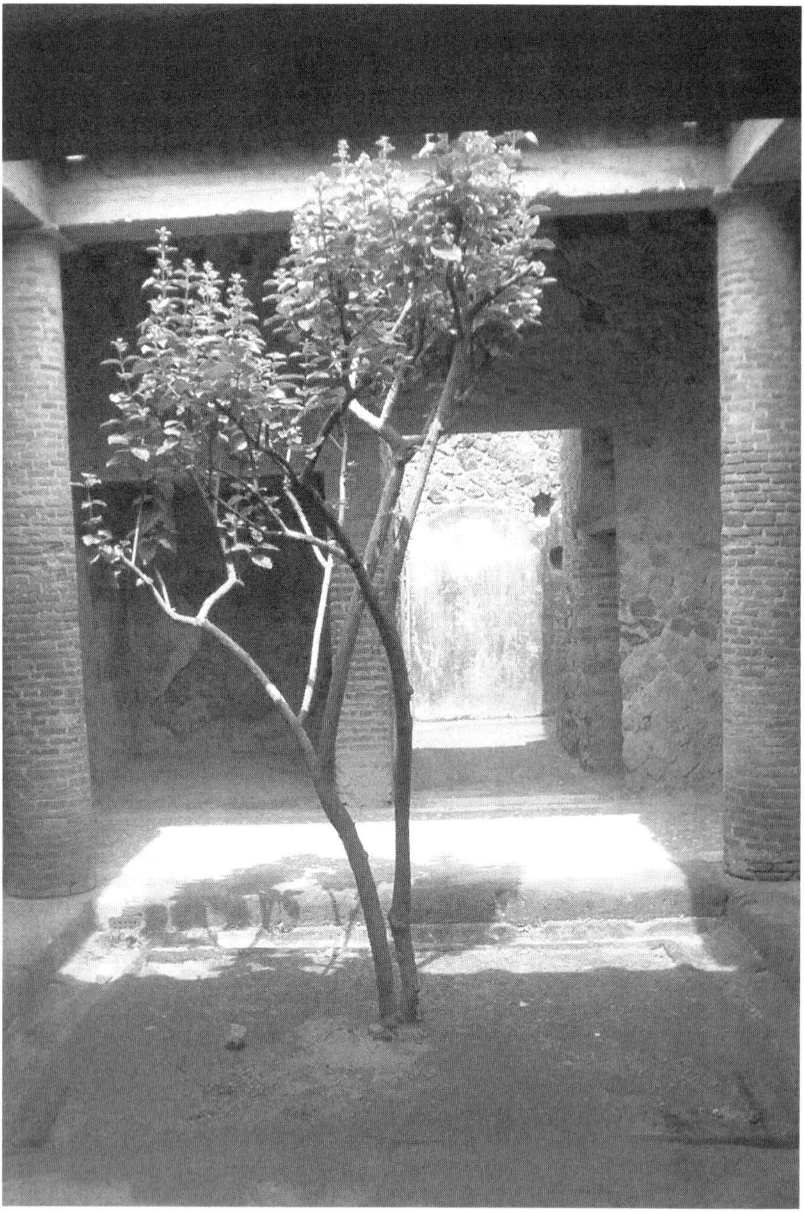

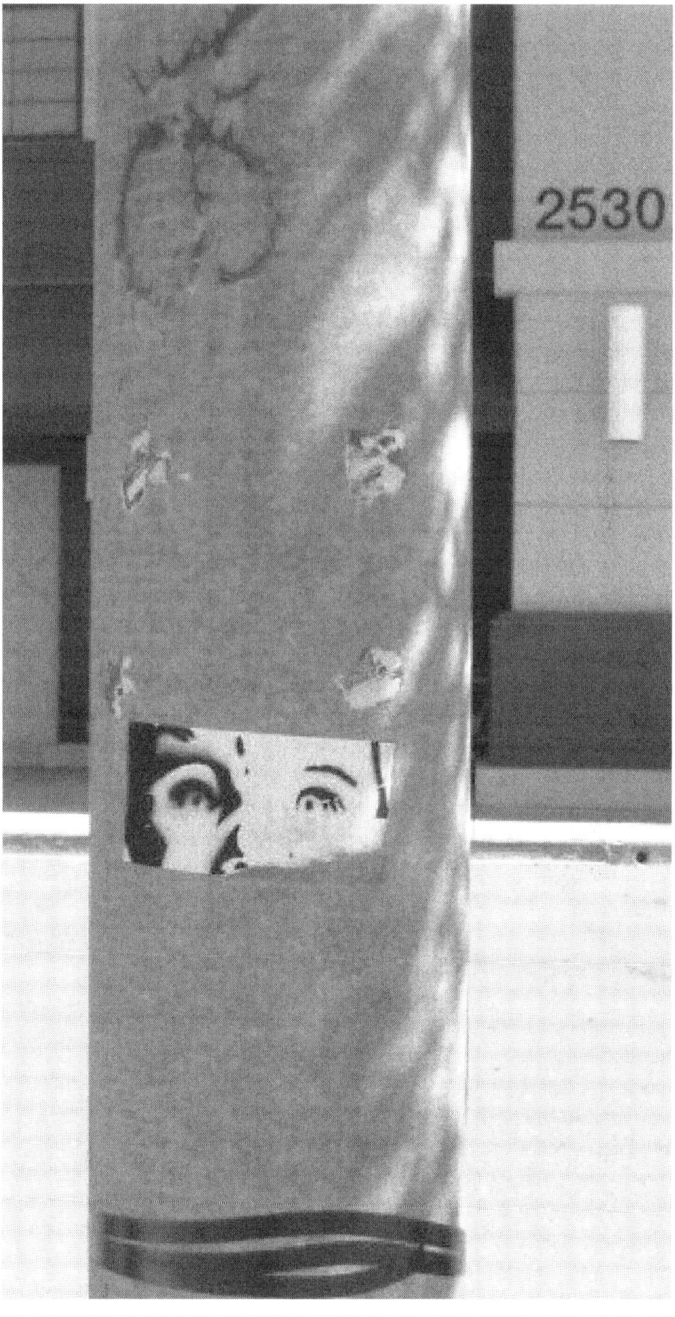
2530

Justin Timberlake And Glitter Glue

We went to the mall's food court today to check out guys.

Afterward we went into the bathroom to throw up.

I have a problem fitting in so I keep Ipecac in my purse.

Date Night

I feel like a bad person.

Maybe not bad, but wrong. I feel that way often when I wonder about what my friends would think if they knew what my interest, or perversion, is. And I can't help but think of them now, as I wait alone in the dark park.

My closest friend has mentioned a few times about wondering what it would like to be with a woman. She's brought it up jokingly to her husband once or twice. I've heard that's a man's dream, but her husband didn't seem interested. She told me that he joked back that they might get one of his male friends to join them. I don't know if he was as serious as she was, but she didn't seem to think so.

One of my friends has been with her boyfriend for many years but has only recently admitted to our small group that she and her boyfriend dabble in SMBD. Sado-Masochism Bondage and Discipline. We all laughed about it and told her it wasn't that crazy, that she could have told us a long time ago. Still, when she isn't around, there are comments or jokes made about it, none in her favor. I myself have made a few of those comments, even some jokes. I don't see the rush or appeal of getting beaten or beating others. Maybe I don't understand though, but I've never thought to ask.

All of us have different interests, not all are so broad. Some of us like big men, some like effeminate men, some are exhibitionists, a few are still virgins. Despite all that, I've never felt able to talk about myself, what I would like to try or what I fantasize about. I wish I could talk to my friends about it, but as it is, I'm alone.

Now I see someone approaching. It could very well not be my date, but all the same I feel my heart begin to race. It doesn't seem to take long before he is right in front of me, and grabs me, and then I know it's him. This is the guy I met on the internet earlier this night. This is the man who has agreed to rape me.

HOLLY
VACANC
NESS
NOV
18
2007
TOWNSEND
Die Fleder
Sunday
2:00
Orchestra Right
Door F4
Floor 2
R 6
$30.00

That's So Me

"That's so me," say millions of kids every day.

How wonderful it must be to see something and be able to say that.

"This is everything I represent and believe."

"Corporations may have groomed me to fit into their styles, but it really is what I would have chosen myself."

I want to find a designer that can represent me. I want to find a celebrity that reflects me.

So far I've been dressing in cotton-polyester blends.

It's what Jerffrey Dahmer wore.

I'm Not A Mother Anymore

I will always associate my baby with the ocean.

Despite all the obvious reasons, her eyes are exactly like the ocean waves. In them is blue, and green, and eternity, and life, and death. The more I think about it, the more she seems the perfect personification of the ocean itself.

Before her, I didn't know life. I didn't know true love, or heartbreak, or emotion. I was floating through my existence, unaware of the fantastic world surrounding me on all sides. Looking back, I don't know how I could have been so blind, but the first time I saw my baby girl, it all changed. She really gave birth to me, and without her I know she's sending me to my grave.

I wish I could change things, but I can't. Some things weren't meant to be, and I wasn't meant to be a mother. God has tried telling me this. My friends and family tried telling me this. Society has tried telling me this. I didn't see it myself until I held her in my arms and realized she was beyond me.

Her eyes, those beautiful ocean eyes, tell me it's okay, and that I'm forgiven. I'm forgiven for letting her cry too long before seeing what she needed. I'm forgiven for being late in feeding her a few times. I'm forgiven for spanking her when I had too little patience to solve a problem on my own. I'm forgiven for putting a little bit of bleach in my own food so she could feel some sort of empathy for me, for a change. She forgives me of all these trivial things, even if no one else will. That's why she's too good for me.

I want to tell her I love her, and I always will. I want to tell her how much she's blessed my life, even in this short period of time. I want to tell her all that she's done for me. But I can't. What words can possibly convey all that? What words that even a toddler would understand? The best I can do is lovingly wash her tiny body one more time, dress her in the pink jumper that makes her look like a cherub, and take her to the ocean for our goodbyes.

She's not crying, she's not smiling. She looks so serene, as if she's sleeping, and I know she is telling me it's going to be all right. I set her down in the bright sand and her jumper makes her stand out like a neon pink ink blot.

"Good," I say, meaning to say "goodbye." but knowing good is more appropriate.

This is a good thing. I will be good after this. She will be good after this.

I hurry to leave in this good moment as the waves pick up to lick at her feet.

I'm leaving her right where she belongs, right where I found her. I can only hope the next woman to walk by will have a more understanding family. One that knows the difference between kidnapping and love.

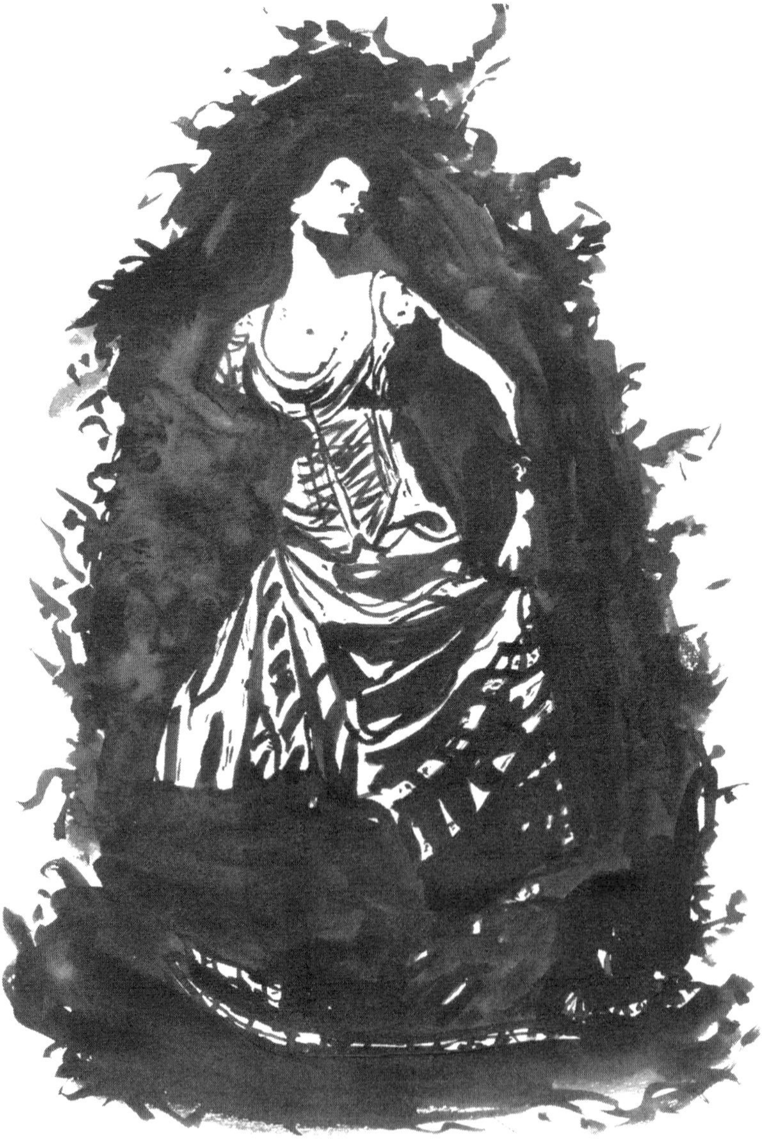

Once Upon A Time

When I was a little girl I used to dream of fairy tale kingdoms with princes and princesses and dragons. I would make up intricate tales of adventure and romance where the prince would over come great odds to rescue the princess. He was as great a hero as anyone had ever created, my prince, and he loved the princess dearly. In the end, the princess always got shot to death.

When I was older I realized there were never guns in fairy tales, I should have stabbed her.

Why do I always get everything wrong?

The Partridge Family, We Are Not

When I was a child, everyone said I would grow up to be a famous singer. I have the looks for it, which is more important than talent if you really look at it. I have the voice for it. I had the drive for it.

I used to perform at local festivals, sporting events, and church. It was a paying job, even before I was old enough to comprehend the transactions fully. I just knew my parents would give me some spending money and put the rest in an account for my college fund. Sometimes I think if I could travel back in time and talk to that innocent girl I was, I would tell her that it doesn't matter how talented, beautiful, or dedicated you are; you need to have practical skills because dreams don't come true.

My life isn't what I imagined, but I'm happy. I'm happy when I'm curled under my blanket at night and I have gotten through another day and have a viable plan to do it again tomorrow. I would rather be beside a husband, or even a lover, at these happy moments, but that isn't my lot in life. I have my son. That's enough.

The focus I used to put on my singing career now goes into caring for him and I've sacrificed enough to be there for him when he comes home from school. I'm there to help him with his homework and cook him dinner and to listen to his day.

This was easier before he entered junior high. The recap of his day used to be childlike and gleeful, if not exasperated. Then it became grim half answers mumbled from a victim's mouth. Now, he doesn't talk about it at all, no matter how much I pry. We both spend our family dinners trying to ignore the swollen tear-stained eyes he avoids looking at me with and the bruises or blood-stained clothes.

I want to go to the school, go to the parents, go to the other children even, but my son begs me adamantly not to. That it would make it worse. That they would call him a fag even more if he was having his mother fight his battles for him.

I've forgotten what it's like to be a child most of the time and I see the situation from a mother's eyes. How can these children bully my son? He's innocent, beautiful, sweet, smart, funny. He's small, helpless, delicate.

I've tried telling him to ignore the taunts. I've told him to tell his teachers. I've told him to fight back. I finally told him to stop giving them reasons to call him gay. I feel guilty for it, but more because I think it's my fault. He's never had a father figure, he inherited my effeminate looks, my love for the arts and singing. Maybe it's my fault he's being called a faggot. Maybe it's my fault that he is one, if kids his age can even have sexuality.

My son wants to be a singer, but I never encourage it. I know that it doesn't matter how talented, beautiful, or dedicated you are; you need to be practical. You need to be realistic. You need to be a man, if you're a man.

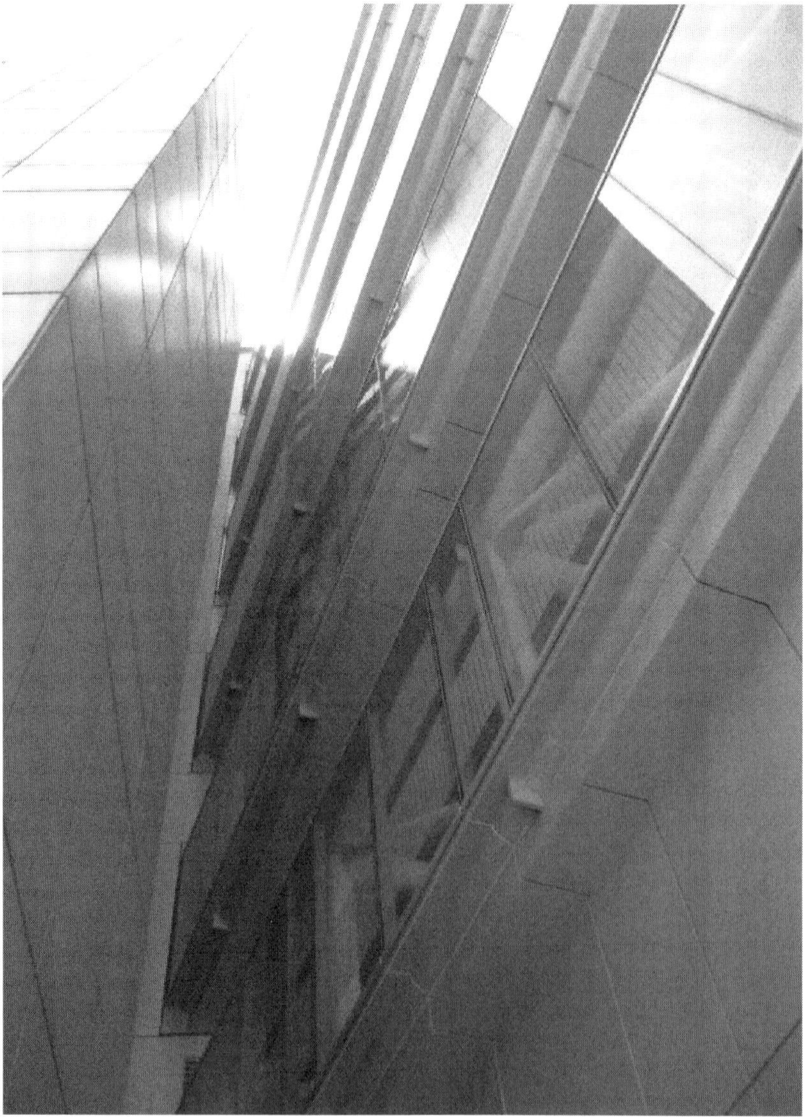

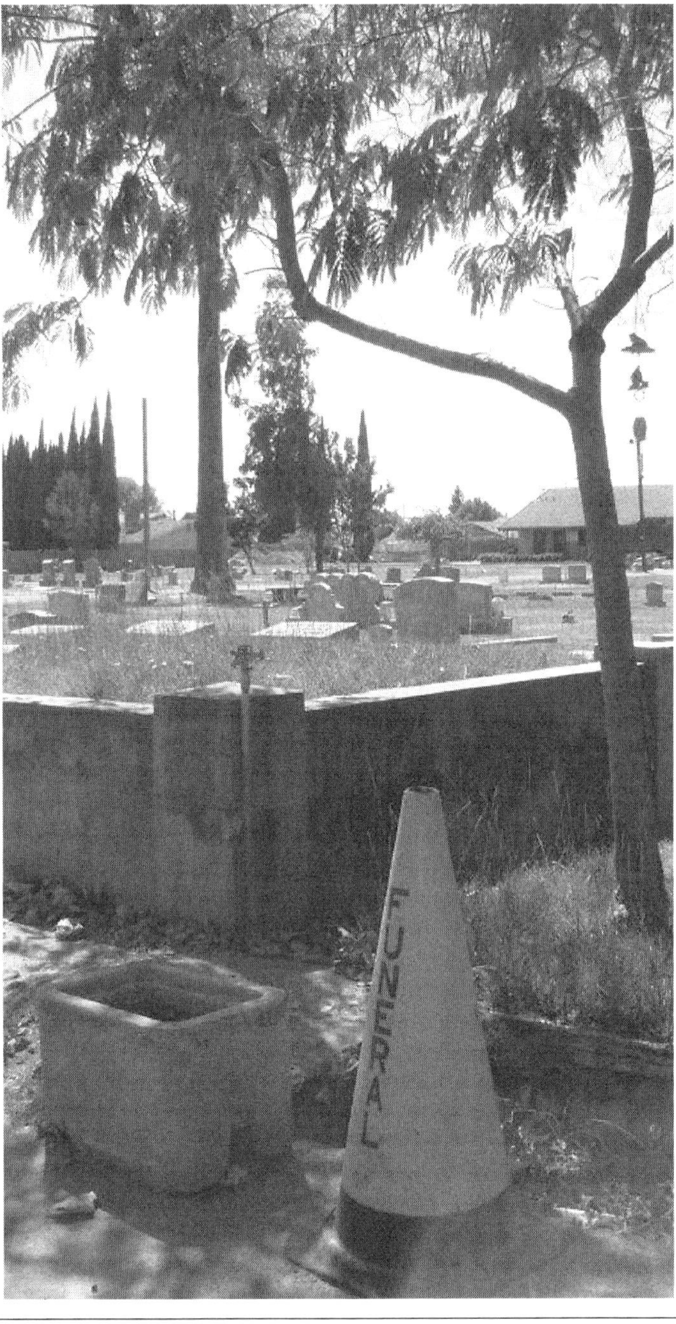
FUNERAL

Because I Love You

I can feel your heart beat against my teeth, and I know you're excited.

I'm excited too.

Being here with you is like a wonderful dream.

You feel the same way, don't you? No one has made you feel the way I do.

Look at you, you can't contain yourself.

Like never before in my life, I'm happy now that I'm here with you.

You'll never know how long I've wanted this.

But you've wanted it to. You must have worried I wouldn't have noticed, but I did. I understand you more then anyone, so you never need to worry again. I'll always understand you.

Your whole body is soft and yielding against mine. It's amazing the way my hands feel against you. My fingers sinking down into the soft creamy skin encasing your inner self, and then down into it.

You must love this as much as I do. Your voice is coming to me louder, faster, desperate.

Don't excite me too much, I want to go slow. I want this to last a long time. For the both of us.

The taste of you is delectable, insatiable, overwhelming.

Salty, then bitter, sometimes metallic. Parts even begin to burn my mouth, but I don't mind. I love all your tastes, I love everything about you.

I'll do anything to feel and taste every part of you. Even if I need to chew through you to get to them.

If your body was a wonder from the outside, it's even more so from the inside.

So soft before, but now so velvety.

This is more then I could have imagined. The feel of you is always changing. When I'm inside it becomes a rush of heat and liquid.

I want to drown in it.

I want to submerge myself into you and breathe you into my lungs, fill my body with yours.

Your skin was so light and ivory colored. Now it's all crimson.

This is your gift to me, isn't it? Because you haven't allowed anyone else to see you like this.

And no one is going to see you like this again.

This can be a moment we'll share forever. This private part of ourselves no one else knows.

You can rest now. You must be tired, because you are so heavy in my arms. I can't see any part of you moving at all.

But that's all right. I'll move for the both of us. I'll breathe for the both of us.

I'll do anything for you, anything at all.

Because I love you.

About The Author

Ms. Stewart was born on March 4, 1985 and raised in Manteca, California. Her name, Christy Leigh Stewart, translates roughly as 'Christian meadow of you-can-take-our-land-but-you-can-never-take-our-freedom'.

She has never done anything of consequence and intends to keep it that way. In her free time she fights for love and justice.

About The Illustrator

Megan Hansen was born and raised in California. She has been working as an illustrator since 2008, and has worked on both adult and children's books.

To order prints of her work visit: etsy.com/shop/meganhansenshop

To contact her, please see her deviant art account: meganhansen.deviantart.com

She's willing to consider any illustration project (as long as it isn't too untoward).

Buy Prints From Megan Hansen

For prints of pieces featured in
this book (in color)
and more!

etsy.com/shop/meganhansenshop

Now Available On Amazon

Familiar Scars

Orphaned, throat slit and left for dead as a child, Orabella struggles to survive with her fellow victim, Rosalyn. She'll grasp at any bit of luck, until it becomes too good to be true.

Mr. Satine is willing to offer his home, heart, and riches over to the beautiful Rosalyn the moment he lays eyes on her. His intentions seem obvious, but become less so when he shows no romantic interest in her, and pure animosity toward Orabella.

Both Orabella and Satine live in their pasts, but what happens when they actually have to confront it?

Satan Is The New Cupid

Halloween; the day the Dying God passes and the year's end comes, the day that begins the dark reign over Earth. The sun sets past the gates of Hell, opening them. For the creatures of the underworld, and the souls awaiting to reenter the world, it's a day of celebration. They are allowed to walk freely on Earth, still hidden by the veil that separates them from the physical realm.

They all have plans, do you?

This books compiles traditional Halloween love spells and rituals along with experimental occultism, chaos magick, and science.

If you can't find love with this book, you might not be lovable.

Printed in Great Britain
by Amazon